Ta

Title	Page
Sarah says hello!! (Sarah Be...	1
Pets, We don't deserve them (Katie Bowman)	3
The No Donation Zone (Sammy Anzer)	7
Tiny Pink and Insignificant (Olivia Schyling)	10
Zeke Saves the Economy (Zeke Herrera)	15
The Doll Hut (Harrison Garcia)	22
Life with Five Dogs...Yes FIVE (Sherri Harper)	25
Letter to Jimmy John (Cory Helie)	29
Thoughts can Run, but They Cannot Hide (Haley Drizcoll)	32
Time Vassal (Cody Ullrich)	34
WEEDEALER303 (James Draper)	40
The New Kid (Mikey Weil)	45
Don't I Know You? (Megan O'Neil)	48
Sex & Gristle (Meghan DePonceau)	53
More Dopamine Please! (Christina Kleemann)	56
Does Feminism Belong in Stand-Up Comedy? (Bridget Callahan)	60
Jesus, That's Weird (Sara B Sirius)	64
The BIBLE: 1 Picture Book w/NO pictures (Colton Dowling)	68
My Precious (Laura Thompson)	74
Baseball & Me (Brad Galli)	78
Kids Say the Darndest Things (Brian Kinney)	82
Deshelled (Steve Vanderploeg)	86
I work at a call center and you can too! (Sarah Benson)	91
Another Day on The Trail (Gabby Gutierrez-Reed)	97
Maria (TC McCracken)	99
How to Start the Best Cult: Netflix Edition (Nate Earl)	101
Drop (Zac Maas)	104
A Review of *About Time* (Joshua Emerson)	109
Quar! Quar! What is it Good for? (Rachel Crowe)	113
Where There's a Will (Billie Jo Gillispie)	118
Mark Masters (Mark Masters)	123
Editor Feedback on COVID-19 Yearbook Spread (Hannah Jones)	127
Cal Observes Things (Cal Sheridan)	129
Join the Undead Legion for better Orgasms (Nyland Vigil)	133
Cranksgiving (Piper Shepherd)	135
Voices You Don't Normally Hear From (Jose Macall)	140
Cute-Ass Cat (Lauren Dufault)	144
My Pony Ran but Stumbled (Ben Bryant)	145
Love in the Time of Covid (Andie Main)	157
Teeny Tiny Chapter 39 (Sarah Benson - last time, I promise!)	166

Why hello there, reader!

Thanks for stopping by! Sarah Benson here, just getting her two cents in before the floodgates of creativity burst open as you peruse the rest of this sweet little book.

All the pieces of this book are written by Colorado comics during a time when live stand-up comedy as we know it was not safe. So instead of slinging jokes to you on a stage, we're bringing you a collection of other things instead! What other things, you ask? You'll just have to skootch your sweet little eyeballs all throughout these pages and find out!

Before you go, I'll give some helpful guidance/directions for reading and enjoying this work of art.

1. Get your imagination ready! Books rely partially on imagination to make them work. It's kind of a "book/imagination buddy-system" that helps the experience move along. The more imagination you use, the better! (Unless you use too much imagination. Then you may find yourself not reading the book at all. You could end up sitting on a beach somewhere surrounded by talking plants [but are you really there or is it just your imagination?])

2. Buckle your seatbelt and get ready to have some fun! This was a little imagination warmup (unless you actually have a seatbelt you buckle when you're about to have a good time.)

3. Take your time and let the contents of this book scoop you up in a blanket and give you a warm hug. This book is meant to be fun! In the battle to make it to the end of an *entire book*, don't forget to enjoy and appreciate the voices of the people whose work you're reading.

4. It's okay if you have to read some parts more than once. (I had to read that sentence 6 times before writing this one!)

5. Follow the contributors on social media! You can even compliment them if you want! Comedians thrive off of compliments. For comedians, compliments provide nourishment and a reason to live.

Alrighty, I think you're probably ready to ride the waves of some peoples' inner thoughts now!

Remember: use your imagination and if there's an emergency, call 9-1-1. And if you accidentally call 9-1-1, stay on the line!

Your pal,

Sarah Benson

Chapter 1

Pets, We don't deserve them

By Katie Bowman

My first thought during quarantine was, "Wow! This would be a great time to adopt a pet."

Then I remembered all the kids in quarantine, just obsessing and over-handling their pets to death. Literally to death and it made me cringe. It made me cringe because I was one of those kids. I have had every pet you could imagine. I'm no Tiger King but I would be lying if I said I have zero pet death's on my record.

I am writing this to say that kids should never be in control of living beings. Ever. They should not be able to have a pet until they can wipe without leaving shit-streak marks in their underwear. They should not be able to own a pet until they know what sex is. Sure you can get them a dog or cat. But that dog or cat should be really owned by the parents. That dog and cat should be very dumb and happy. Don't buy a dog or cat because of its breed (you asshole.) Buy a random rescue puppy or kitty that doesn't know harm or get a slappy silly goofball also from a shelter. Because that dog or cat will endure some serious damage. Damage that most other pets (lizards, snakes, birds, fish.) won't be able to live through. And if your hypothetical dogs and cats ever bite or scratch your kid you better find them a new home and not just give them the Green Mile Walk by signing the papers.

People personify pets unlike anything I have ever seen before. People prefer cats to dogs, dogs to cats and they also decide to own whatever pet they want and the minute these pets are in a place where they are attacking a human they get put down. Zoo animals are no exception to this either. RIP Harambe.

I don't know what it is about mankind feeling like we have to dominate other living creatures. I see people walking their dogs off leash like it's some flex. They want to showcase how well-behaved of a dog they have as if the dog isn't also in danger from other dogs and cars. I see people clipping bird's wings, and modeling with dead game. It is a lot and at the end of the day we think these creatures need our companionship. Nope. They can do fine without us.

I want to come clean of all the poor pets that endured me as a kid. My first ever known pet was Lizzie Bitsy Bowman. She was a Jack Russel Terrier and she was divine. She had a beautiful paint-like coat and was just so playful. The poor thing was obsessed with my mom. She didn't give a flying fuck about any of the kids and why would she. We would always dress her up in stuff, take her away from her queen (my mom), give her too many baths and make her hump stuff (she would hump our legs and we would laugh). I don't blame her for biting me every single time. Lizzie would bite me and I would weap to my mom and my mother would say, "you shouldn't have been taunting her." I am so thankful that my mom taught me how to act around dogs and cats. I see many idiots just running up to dogs expecting an embrace and the dog abruptly tells them to F off.

Liz was a great dog. She endured a lot but no child trauma death for that lucky pup. She lived to be fourteen and was an amazing bitch.

I had a million fish, oh the poor fish. I thought you could pet fish, like actually pet them. So as you already know, they all died. I had hamsters. The pet store told us they were same gendered but they were wrong. Isn't that hilarious? My hamsters mated and just kept mating with all their incestious offspring and eventually we had like over forty of those little devils. They became vicious little creatures and they eventually ate the original mother (yikes). At that point my mom was so fed up with the smell and just incest hamsters she took them back to the pet store. The pet store said no refunds but she told them they could sell the larger ones and then use the pinkies as snake food AND THEY TOOK THEM BACK. What a nightmare.

I had lizards that I also got from pet shops and I would also catch lizards on family vacations and of course I would aggravate them. Then they would open their mouths as a defense mechanism to scare me away in which I figured out how to put their open mouth next to my tongue and ears which then triggered them to bite the area and dangle like an earring. I then walked around the hotel scaring old ladies with lizards hanging from my face. I was an odd kid. All of the lizards died from over handling.

Lots of caught turtles, frogs, crawfish as well. I also had two box turtles that ran away. I am not kidding, I lost the turtles in our yard.

Rabbits were a fun time, they pooped too much and my mom gave them to a farm. One died.

I had a bunch of hermit crabs that also all died from over handling or we simply didn't know what we were doing. Probably both.

We saw the movie Polly and I had to get a couple cockatoos. Turns out they also weren't same sex so they had three chicks. And remember, I don't know what sex is at this age so I would watch them have bird sex and be like "is he hurting her?" We let them fly around the house so much and poop everywhere my mom gave them away. Can you blame her?

I caught a baby duckling once. I told my mom I found it. I tried to shower with it and sleep with it like in Fly Away Home and I smothered it to death. Not the worst part. I then let my mom take the blame for its death for twenty-nine years. She to this day brought it up enough that I finally came clean. I was so full of shame.

I was a weird kid. One of the only redheads in my weird little Dallas school - which didn't make it any easier.. I always thought animals and nature were way cooler than people and I just wanted to be a part of their world. I didn't understand doing less is more and simply admiring an animal is better than touching. I didn't understand the concept of life, love and death. It's a terrifying place to be for a pet. If you're a parent and you want a pet you have to do your research. Be responsible and teach your kid how to act, but you have to know that the pet you bought is really your pet. Take care of it, and don't take it to a shelter the first time something goes a little askew.

In college, I had my last weird pet. Aside from my outdoor cat, Kaya who I had to find a better home for due to a sketchy neighbor threatening him but I won't get into that story.

Anyway, I bought some snakes. I always wanted a snake as a kid. But my parents weren't into it but when I got to college I was like NOW, I CAN. Petsmart was literally selling pythons for twenty-five dollars (WHAT A DEAL). I went thrifting and found an aquarium. I bought the snake before the aquarium. No idea why. Then the aquarium got sold, couldn't afford a real tank so I bought a storage bin and poked holes in it until I could figure it out. Smart, I know. Guess what though, the snake wasn't having it and ran away! Classic Katie. So, how did I handle my snake running away? I bought another snake of course. A year later I had moved out of the house I was living in and the girl who had moved in found the first snake in a bathroom. My dumbass was like, "excuse me, that's mine." And I took it back. The snake wasn't acclimated to shelter again and died of starvation. I then enrolled in an anthropology course and learned the behavior of snakes and It was clear I had to give it away.

That one class taught me a lot. Animals are tough, you should get one only if you're truly ready, educated and dedicated to it. Remember what is a pet and what isn't. If you think you want it, go paint a picture of it or just take a picture. Stop feeding the birds Debbie! Adopt your pets and remember to ask to pet them. Finally, please remember not to leave them in your kid's possession!

Yours truly,
Katie Bowman

Webstie: www.KatieBowman.Rocks
Instagram: MissKatieBowman
Twitter: KatieBowmanSays

Chapter 2

The No Donation Zone

By Sammy Anzer

A homeless guy asked me for money, so I flipped open my wallet and gave him the singles I knew I had left. On the next block, I saw a dude playing the drums and he gave me a look like, "Come on man, help me out," but I let him know about the more conveniently placed homeless man. But at the same damn time--another eager dude started begging me to sign a petition about wolves. I was starting to feel harassed. Until I saw this fiiiine woman. Fine.

So I got ready to pivot wolf-petition-boy and go kick game to her, but then I realized, Wait. This is how she feels all the time. Every day, conveniently placed men approach her and try to get something out of her.

Because if you're a woman and some dude hits on you with a variation of Hey lemme have your number--or you're a man and someone hits you with a variation of Hey, lemme get a dollar--either way part--just part of you--thinks, "Shit! How do I get out of this?"

And here's the thing: I give money to people on the street. But I also cross the street when I see those people on the corner with iPads supporting a cause. Good for you, Doctors Without Borders, but try to make money without making me zigzag home like I'm avoiding MS-13.

And we feel that way even if we're down for their cause: the environment, gay rights, food banks, whatever—it's still just a little uncomfortable. And that's because you know the only reason they're talking to you is to get something out of you.

And, in a weird way, it makes you feel cheap. You feel less like a person and more like a walking resource to be exploited. Like that free Redbull truck. You don't even care who's driving it just gimme the free shit you feel me.

Women know how it feels, but men--we gotta use our

imagination. What if people didn't just ask you for money in the street? They asked you for it in coffee shops while you were figuring out the tip, they asked you for it in the gym while you were sweating to Sports Center and mastering the stair, they would even ask you for it while you were in Walgreens, in your dirty sweats, by the always-on-sale vitamins.

"Damn! Can I pick out my Dr. Scholl's in peace!? I don't know if I want arch support or Tri-Comfort yet!

You would think but wouldn't say.

Because the guy hitting you up doesn't read social cues. And If he's going to make that move while you're in the middle of feeling up inserts, he also doesn't handle rejection well. So say something nice--but not too nice--and get back to your possibly accredited podiatrist.

And that guy's not looking for a sole mate.

I'll stop.

OK, no I won't.

People would start meaningful conversations with you and end them by asking for money. Friends you spent years with would reveal to you that they actually wanted money, and when you didn't give it to them, boom, the friendship was over. They would always say something that came down to: I thought we had something special. I thought you'd be the one to give me money but you put me in the "no donation zone."

I don't owe you anything!

Again, you would think but wouldn't say.

You become so good at picking up on when someone wants money from you that you can see them asking with their eyes. You catch people ogling your wallet daily. And then you become numb to it. It happens so much that you stop being friendly with people and stop making eye contact with them. They resent you for it; they're like, "You don't have to donate anything, but could you at least smile?"

But five motherfuckers a day have been asking you for money everywhere you go, every day since you were fifteen. And sometimes, when you tried to turn them down nicely, they'd explode

"I don't even want your money! You broke anyway, bitch!"

That's why you stopped smiling on the street.

So, I didn't hit on that fiiiine woman or ask her for her number. But I did stop. And look at her, and said, "Hey can I have a dollar?"

Instagram: BadBoyAnzer

Chapter 3

Tiny Pink and Insignificant

By Olivia Schyling

"Just so you guys know, the walls are leaking, and we might need to scale off the balcony if the wall bursts," B.J said matter of factly.

It was comforting to have someone so confident in a crisis. The water had been coming through the crack under the door even though we had put sandbags in front, and now through the cracks in between the tiles in the bathroom. The floor was entirely covered in water and it was only getting higher. So we did the only thing we could do to keep the water from completely overtaking the apartment. We started scooping water into 5-gallon buckets, tubs bowls and anything we could find and dumping them into the bathtub.

I was squatting, staying out of the way of my two friends, Dane and Carson. As they waddled by with another full 5 gallons to dump in the bathtub. I had chosen to fend off the water with a dustpan and a thin-lipped plastic Tupperware lid. Whereas Amber armed herself with a mop. No matter how fast we worked the water just kept coming. With our backs sore and soaked in dirty water, we started taking breaks in shifts, until we all could take one during the eye of the storm.

. . .

I had moved to the Virgin Islands from Colorado only 7 weeks before the first hurricane hit. Initially for some promising commercial and independent film gigs, with the bonus of a beautiful island backdrop. I had been signed on to do makeup on an independent film the day that Irma hit, as well as having a training session as a barista for an adorable seaside combo coffee shop deli 2 days prior.

Things didn't work out the way I'd expected. I never saw the owner of the shop who had hired me after the training nor got to work on any of the things I thought I would. Although we have hours and hours of footage, some for our own personal use, some we eventually sold for news coverage. We taped the hurricane itself, or what we could capture, then our lives after the hurricanes and how drastically things changed.

We overheard that there was going to be a category 3 hurricane, (which would later turn into a category 5) heading our way which explained why people were whipped up in a frenzy and stocking up on the necessities. So, we switched gears and started getting the essentials.

There were still a few days until Irma hit. So, we spent that time prepping as best as one can when God herself is sending a storm on par with the genesis flood. We were building our own arc by nailing 2 x 4s on the windows and doors of our newly rented apartment.

When we asked our landlord if he could get the hurricane shutters out of storage, he said it would be more work than it was worth. And at that time the entire complex was undergoing renovations, so there were lots of planks, boards and other dangerously loose debris. We took it upon ourselves to try to protect the place with the very things that would otherwise be launched 180 mph at it.

Even with the windows boarded up, we knew we couldn't seek refuge from the storm there. That's when we heard a rumor about a well-known hotel chain that was housing people through the storm in the ballrooms in the basement. We heard it through a friend of a friend which goes to show you to check your sources.

Because at 6 in the morning the day of the storm, we got kicked out and locked outside of that well-known hotel chain just as the wind was starting to kick up. With no place to go, we called our good friends B.J and Lizzy, asking for one big favor, if they could take us in during the storm. Later they would have us over for the second hurricane and for the false alarm of the 3rd hurricane, Jose, that was supposed to hit in that 3 week period but ended up going north and missing the Caribbean islands. They were our guardian angels and I still wonder how we would have survived without them.

We still had to get to the safe house which was clear across the island, and the storm was licking our heels. The drive was intense, and in my memory I could swear I could see the storm taking shape, touching down and chasing after us. It was a dark morning and the electricity was vibrating through everything and everyone. We were all nervous, with nothing we could say to each other that would be of any comfort, we rode in silence.

Bj and Lizzy's place was perched perfectly on the top of a hill with the best view of the rest of the island . They were also watching the apartment under theirs for a boat captain friend. They frequently dog sit and were currently watching a big slobbery mastiff, named Simon with a blue bandana that made him look like Scooby doo, though he was twice as jumpy. He was a welcome member to our little ragtag group.

The storm was just getting started, stretching, yawning compared to what was coming. The power cut out within a few hours and would be off for the next 8 months. We had evacuated the upstairs apartment earlier in fear that the wooden roof was going to fly off. It was already peeling up around the edges, and happening to houses all over the island that very instant. We moved caravan style, all holding hands to get to the apartment on the floor below. It was now light and very loud outside. Everything around us was fighting an invisible foe, that was trying to shake, break or uproot anything it came across.

We made it to the downstairs apartment, set up the mosquito repellant lanterns and flashlights to give us the most light possible. The ceiling and all the walls were cement, which felt like a safe haven that could crush us if things went wrong. I appreciated the cold muffled change of scenery but was less than happy with the new heightened sensations of the vibrations being held in by the thick walls.

 The hurricane shutters on the glass doors were huge and blocked out most of the light. They were made of dark wood that made them look medieval. Whenever wind shot in between the glass and the wood it would make a howling sound, which sometimes sounded like a high pitched woman's scream, other times it sounded like a haunted ghost train. The wind was so powerful it would rip and tear, then heave sink, and wind up again.

We tried to get some sleep before the wind got up to the guaranteed 150 mph, which later would surpass at 185 mph. We were only getting the southwestern part of the eye, with the shape of the storm it meant it would be a short time for us until the wall of the back of Irma hit us. We had another 6 hours to go.

I don't remember who noticed but thank goodness one of us did. The floor was wet. Not a good sign. We had to act fast. We tried stuffing the cracks with rags, towels and blocking with sandbags, which only helped slow things down. That's when we started manually scooping the water and dumping it in the bathtub in an attempt to keep the water at bay.

We continuously cleared out the water for about 6 or 7 hours, only really getting a break during the eye of the storm. It was one of the most eerily peaceful things I have ever experienced.

After hours upon hours of howling, shaking, and tearing. Things seemed silent. When we opened the door, I really didn't know what to expect. I first noticed the smell of it all. It smelt like mulch and already like things were rotting. The first thing we saw was a car bumper stuck in the stairwell. Cautiously we ventured from our hidey hole into the new upturned world. The driveway had become a cascading waterfall.

The once lush green island had turned brown, all the green had been stripped away. The ocean was the brightest blue I had ever seen. Even though up close, it was actually murky with all the sand that had been shaken up like a tropical snow globe. There was patio furniture stuck in trees. We found an injured iguana under a fallen tree down the road, we named her Irma and took her in until she could take care of herself in the wild, just as she healed so did the island.

We would go on to document the effects and destruction of the island, as well as the close community charged by the events, and the bonds created by them. By the time we woke up the next day the roads were being cleared, houses were being swept of the water and debris. The healing process had begun.

Every stranger was immediately a new friend, wanting to hear about your family, how your home held up, and if there was anything they could do to help. The island hadn't missed a beat. Things kept moving, houses got rebuilt, restaurants gave meals to those in need, family and friends were brought closer together, and this was just the first hurricane. By the time Maria came around, we were veterans. After all that I realized how tiny, pink and insignificant I am. So hold your loved ones close, give a hand when you can and take one when you need one.

Instagram: Olivia_Schyling

Chapter 4

Zeke Save the Economy

By Zeke Herrera

I'm a man that keeps a tight schedule.

8:00 am: wake up.
9:00 am: get out of bed and get dressed.
12:00 pm: realize I woke up too early, take a nap.
5:00 pm: get out of bed.
6:00 pm: spanish practice.
7:00 pm: Jazzercise.
7:05 pm: listen to jazz music.
7:30 pm: go to a stand up comedy open mic, bomb.
11:00 pm: drive home only to realize my neighbor Adrian parked in my parking spot again.
12:00 am: find parking, fist fight Adrian.
1:00 am: watch tv until I fall asleep.

One morning, I wake up in my bed to a fluorescent light piercing through my eyelids. I look around my bed to see my familiar picture covered walls had been replaced with blank metal ones.

I open the door to a large hallway covered in red carpeting. The walls are littered with giant portraits in gold frames and marble statues. A man is walking towards me that looks identical to whatever you've been imagining I look like up to this point. He's wearing a very expensive suit but he definitely doesn't seem as cool as me.

Me: Are you me from the future?

President Zeke: Hahahahahahahahhaha! That's funny, I guess our file was wrong about you but no. God no. I'm you from a parallel universe where I'm The President of the United States of America.

Me: What the hell is going on?

President Zeke: I've brought you here to help solve the economic crisis on this earth.

Me: I'm the key to solving everything?

President Zeke: Oh, God, no. You're basically our control group. You're smart enough to understand what we're saying and dumb enough to where we can get an accurate gauge of the public's reaction. How did your last fight with Adrian go?

Me: He's got a colonoscopy scheduled for my boot next week. How about yours?

President Zeke: Unfortunately I was disqualified for substance abuse issues.

Me: Steroids?

President Zeke: Flubber. Listen, we need to fix this economy. It's failing and nobody has any idea why.

Me: What'd you do?

President Zeke: *sighs* I tried to institute mandatory orgies. Which is a GREAT idea on paper but it turns out it is not actually as cool as I thought and hard to enforce.

Me: Have you tried stopping the orgy law?

President Zeke: *whispering to an assistant* Get that taken care of.

We walk into the oval office, a litany of Zekes fill the room. They're mostly chatting amongst each other but some are making out and fist fighting, respectively.

President Zeke: Let's get you introduced to everybody. Hey everybody! This is regular Zeke! We're going to go around the room and introduce ourselves. Just say your thing and a little something about yourself.

Celebrity Zeke: Hi, I'm famous. I have two Emmys, three Oscars and a Pulitzer that I made into a chain. I've had sex with too many celebrities to list but what the heck let's give it a shot. Awkwaf...

President Zeke: We get the point. Anybody else?

Boy Genius Zeke: I used to just be a regular Zeke but one day a chemical waste truck collided with a school bus and...

President Zeke: Right, I forgot you have a whole origin story. Okay, this was a terrible idea. So we have Celebrity Zeke, Boy genius Zeke, Ghost Zeke, Union Zeke, Caveman Zeke, Conspiracy Zeke, Pirate Zeke, Stripper Zeke, Monk Zeke and Lasagna Zeke.

Me: Wait everyone gets a thing but me!? Pirate Zeke isn't even that piratey.

Pirate Zeke: Argh! I be a lawyer in mi universe. We just has a penchant for the nautical.

Me: What about Lasagna Zeke? Are you from some lasagna universe?

Lasagna Zeke: That doesn't make any sense. What's a lasagna universe? I just really like lasagna.

Me: I like lasagna!

Stripper Zeke: Yeah but it's HIS thing.

Me: It's Garfield's thing! I do stand up, I can be Stand Up Zeke! Or Narrator Zeke?

Conspiracy Zeke: Famous Zeke has an Emmy for Stand Up, an Oscar for narrating and gills behind his shoulder blades.

President Zeke: Look you're just the most regular out of all of us. We brought you in as a control group to see how all the other average people would take our ideas. We don't really care about your opinions.

Me: My opinions matter less than Caveman Zeke's?

President Zeke: His economy is actually doing pretty well. They just still have dinosaurs and live in caves. He also speaks the most Español out of all of us.

Caveman Zeke: No tenemos hacerlo chunga una competencia chaka.

President Zeke: For where he comes from. We can call you "Weiner Zeke" cause you're being a weiner right now. Now sit your ass down! We need to fix this economy

Union Zeke: Let's create some jobs and pay the workers a liveable wage.

President Zeke: And who's going to pay them? Me and Famous Zeke? NEXT!

Ghost Zeke: Weee coooouuuuld hiiiiire peeeeoplllle to solve every murder.

Stripper Zeke: Sounds reasonable.

Famous Zeke: And incriminating.

President Zeke: Not if it's legal for you.

Union Zeke: Nobody needs to be looking into which kinds of bodies are at what type of construction sites. What if we start selling our oil to other people?

Pirate Zeke: I got me barrels handy!

Lasagna Zeke: Seems like it might cause some spillage.

Union: Then we'll just pay people to clean it up! It's a win win!

Caveman Zeke: What's oil kachunga?

Ghost Zeke: Whhhhoooo'sss gooooiing tooo tell hiiim?

Stripper Zeke: It's like gas

Boy Genius Zeke: We'll need a new more efficient mode of transportation. Might I recommend making sidewalks into trampolines?

Conspiracy Zeke: Or we turn down gravity in the simulation

Monk Zeke: We must learn to let go of our worldly possessions.

Stripper Zeke: So you can buy more later

Famous Zeke: Can I still keep the moon rocks Buzz Aldren gave me? They're not worldly.

Boy Genius: If I could actually get my hands on those. I'm building an antigravity gun.

Me: I'm positive it does not work like that.

President Zeke: It does!

12 pm rolls around we all fall asleep. I wake up to a field of unconscious doppelgangers and go shake the president.

Me: Wake up!

President Zeke: Oh shit it's almost six o'clock! ¡Necesitamos practicar Español ahora!

Me: We don't have time dude!

President Zeke: En Español por favor.

Me: ¡No tengo tiempo wey!

Caveman Zeke:*tenemos ooka

Me: I've just never conjugated about duplicates of me yet.

President Zeke: Solo haz lo mejor que puedas

Me:

President Zeke: Just do the best you can

Me: I was getting there

Stripper Zeke: *Estaba llegando allí

Me: Right ¿"derecha"?

Pirate Zeke: *"estribor"

Boy Genius Zeke: *"Correcto"

Me: Derecha, gracias.

Jazzercise time finally comes around but we find out that none of us actually know how to Jazzercise. We've all just been guessing this whole time. So there we are, a sea of uncoordinated flailing and finger shakin'. After that we did an open mic in The Oval Office. We all try out our new economy based material that we saved because we didn't want to waste it on the pitch meeting. Everything gets pitched from Monk and Ghost Zekes' more spiritual and enlightened ideas to Conspiracy and Celebrity Zekes' more antisemetic and icthyophobic media controlling ideas. It all bombs because we're all looking at our phones except for Pirate Zeke who we all pay attention to only because he really found that blackout drunk sweet spot.

After the open mic is over the president loads us all up into Air Force One and I eventually realize he's taking us to fight Adrian. I asked him where we were going to fight Adrian and if you're a Zeke reading this you'll never believe it but that piece of shit is the goddamn King of England. Every night they trade off going to each other's home turfs and duke it out surrounded by thousands of spectators.

We arrive and start to get lowered into the colosseum only to realize that Adrian also brought in Adrians from parallel universes but since England has universal healthcare it wasn't plummeted into poverty by the orgies that Adrian threw because people had access to chlamydia medication and safe abortions. So Adrian didn't need a braintrust and brought in all the toughest Adrians from all the most badass universes. We're toast. Just as our platform lands I hear a voice yell out.

Lasagna Zeke: What if we just made it illegal to hoard money!? Just one person isn't allowed to have cartoonish/unfathomable stockpiles of money anymore. We need to spread the ricotta out to keep some sauce in every bite and to make sure the meat is covered if it needs to see a chef. I know it's going to be hard for Celebrity Zeke and to a lesser extent President Zeke and Pirate Zeke and I know it won't fix everything but it's just a base in which to lay our noodles.

Everybody dies.

The End.

Twitter and Instagram: MurderMtnDew

Chapter 5

The Doll Hut

By Harrison Garcia

"Are you on drugs right now?", he asked before running to the bathroom to throw up again. Hours earlier we had made the decision to cancel our set at the Doll Hut in Anaheim; a show for which we had driven from Denver, with stops to play at an amazing sounding venue for less than 10 people in Salt Lake City, a very close-call with police in Park City, the threat of the opening band robbing us in Oakland, a disappearing soundman in a basement in San Francisco, and our singer taking ecstasy then wandering off during our set in Santa Cruz.

It was our first time playing outside of Denver, and booking the entire thing using Google and leads from friends had been no small feat. But after mailing out posters to venues, praying they would hang them up, quitting our terrible service industry jobs, and spending countless hours hammering out a style of indie-electronic music that we were convinced would change the world, we were as ready as could be.

The drummer's parents' Isuzu Trooper loaded up with gear didn't get great gas mileage, but was our only option since between the three of us we only had one car and two valid driver licenses. He was the only one who knew how to drive a stick, and after attempts to teach me proved unsuccessful, would end up driving the entire way himself. Trooper indeed. The day we left Denver for a two-week run, our singer and main songwriter showed up with all his worldly possessions in a garbage bag and no cell phone. At that point in our relationship as a band, it was in no way a surprise.

The night before the show at The Doll Hut, we had slept on a beach along Highway 1 then eaten at a burrito joint when got to LA. None of us had eaten a California burrito before, which is just a regular burrito with fries and guacamole thrown in it. It was so tasty and affordable on our meager budget, but the next day proved to be a massive mistake when two of us got very sick. If you're ever in LA, I do not recommend Burrito King in Silverlake.

Shortly before leaving for the tour I'd spent months planning, a doctor told me to get my tonsils taken out as soon as possible if I didn't want to keep getting strep throat. Earlier that year, I had played the band's very first show while battling a high fever and swollen throat. When I told the doctor that as soon as possible wasn't going to happen, they gave me antibiotics and told me to take it easy. The only reason I didn't get sick from those burritos was either because I have a digestive system made of steel, or because of the antibiotics. Pretty sure it was the antibiotics.

After arriving at a hotel that my Dad had mercifully arranged, I made the necessary calls and emails to let the venue know that we weren't going to make it. But since I felt fine, had booked the other acts myself, and sitting in a hotel while my bandmates violently expelled their insides didn't seem fun, I decided to go check out the show.

I still couldn't drive a stick shift, so I walked the few miles to the venue. Of all the places we booked, The Doll Hut was the one I was most looking forward to because it's one of those legendary hole in the walls where bands played before they went onto smooth out their sound and get rich and famous.

After meeting people who I had only previously spoken to via email and sending my apologies on behalf of the rest of my sick band, I claimed a stool at the bar. There were very few people in the crowd as the opening act, a DJ in S&M leather whose sound I can best describe as Nine-Inch-Nails-lite, started the show.

After a few songs, a guy at the bar asked if I knew when the headliner would be on. I took a beat because I was certain that he somehow knew and was playing a cruel joke. Turns out that he lived close, checked us out online, and bought a ticket to the show; which is, and I cannot stress this enough: exactly what a new band on the road for the first time wants to have happen.

I explained the situation and apologized while giving him a download card with the EP we finished a day before leaving. He asked if we would still be able to make our final shows in Phoenix and Albuquerque, and I told him I could only hope the other guys would recover by tomorrow. At the end of our conversation, he asked, in the casual manner of a man who had definitely been generous with strangers before, "Well... want some acid?"

I was 22 years old, in California on my first tour as a musician who played bass guitar through a Moog synthesizer. I wasn't about to insult him.

This was how I came to be walking past Disneyland around midnight on a Sunday while tripping. Hard. Upon returning to the hotel, my drug-fueled brain immediately picked up the sick vibes the guys were very strongly emitting. Once the thought got in my head that I still had toxic food inside of me, my relatively chill trip turned dark quickly. I became convinced that I had to get it out of me or I would become irreversibly, permanently sick, and soon enough started to vomit.

I was in the bathroom when I heard our drummer quietly laughing at me, and I knew it was all going to be OK.

Instagram: Harrison_Gramica
Facebook: Harrison.Garcia

Chapter 6

Life with Five Dogs...Yes FIVE

By Sherri Harper

After two marriages that had run their course and then enduring multiple dating nightmares as a single woman, I decided to commit my life to dogs. IMy obsession began with one dog, Walter, and I needed more company so that's when I rescued "the twins'." Jack and Gus had been transported to Colorado from Texas where they had been found running the streets after a hurricane. They were residing in my local animal shelter and had been there for months. They needed to stay together and that was more than some people wanted to take on. But I needed a lot of dogs to fill the eternal void in my soul, so it was a perfect fit!

Then in walks Mr. Right. We met through Facebook in part because we both love dogs. Neither of us had planned to ever love another human being yet here we were. In LOVE. He has two. Stewie the Pug and Rocky the 3-legged terrier of some sort.. We were married within six months and that's how we ended up with 5 dogs...500 dogs...5 million dogs. Keep in mind we only have 4 hands between the two of us so having 5 dogs is absolutely ridiculous. When they all want attention at the same time SOMEONE has to settle for a foot.

So, let me introduce you to our pack. Walter is Top Dog. He is 11 years old and looks like a miniature cattle dog mixed with a chihuahua. GIANT ears. Sadly, he was recently diagnosed with cancer. When things go wrong in life, my go-to phrase is "Well, at least it's not ass cancer"...only THIS time it was. Ass cancer. He did not respond well to the initial treatment and was miserable, so we discontinued treatment. We are just keeping him comfortable and taking cues from him. He has been doing well overall. His breed can only be described as "being a Walter". He looks like he is a cross between a small cattle dog and a chihuahua. He is a walking middle finger, gives zero fucks and won't tolerate anyone's shit. He is grumpy and smart. He knows how to open the dog blockade and let the others into places they are not supposed to be. He is the self-appointed referee of the pack and keeps everyone in check. He is defiant and will absolutely ignore any commands that he doesn't want to do. He also thinks he is part human and that when we eat dinner, he needs to partake with us. And let's face it, we are suckers and the dude has ass cancer, so we give him some.

Next in line is Stewie. Stewie is a Pug. He is 8 years old. I'm not sure if you have ever met a Pug but they are just weird...totally adorable but weird. He whines about everything. He has these googly eyes that point in different directions so you can never be 100% who he is looking at. He also must lick your leg for no less than 5 minutes several times a day. Stewie didn't get neutered until this past year because my husband thought he might get into the breeding business. When I met him, I told him how stupid that idea was and so chop chop for Stewie. This loss of testicles has turned him into a chubby kid...I'm talking about Stewie, not my husband. Stewie thinks he needs a third breakfast everyday. I have to watch that kid like a hawk to make sure he doesn't overeat. I swear if he could access the pantry I would find him covered in Cheetos dust. The Pug always needs to have you in his sightline and, as a thank you, his asshole will always be in your sightline. He has one of those curly tails, so his butt always looks like it has a question. I see his asshole so many times during the day that I now think of my third eye as a Pug asshole. Namaste.

After Stewie and his asshole is Rocky. Rocky is a 3 year old terrier of some sort. He is pure white and has wiry hair and chocolate colored eyes that will melt your face right off. He was born with a misshapen paw. My husband adopted him knowing he would need aggressive physical therapy and lots of patience. He worked with him for over a year and sadly Rocky did not respond well and started trying to chew off his own curled little paw. The vet recommended amputation and that is how Rocky became a tripod. He does just fine without that troublesome paw and is the happiest most loving dog I have ever met. He gives hugs. He literally gives HUGS. He is so sweet that he just started a new job as the emotional support dog at the urgent care where my husband works.

Finally, the twins. They are also 3 years old and are Chiweenies. I call them my rat babies. Hence, the name choice. They look like giant white mice. Cinderella's mice were named Jack and Gus. And since I have so much in common with Cindy, I thought it was fitting. Still waiting for woodland creatures to clean my house when I sing out a window, but I digress. So far the only tasks Jack and Gus perform is a good floor cleaning if I drop some scraps off of the kitchen counter. We will get there....fingers crossed. When I first got the twins, they were PAINFULLY shy. I could barely touch them without them quivering. After 2 years, Jack has come out of his shell quite a bit. He is still a bit timid but will allow you to pick him up and snuggle him. Gus, on the other hand, is afraid of his own farts.

All the dogs sleep in bed with us except Gus. He sleeps under the bed and then when we turn the lights out will jump onto the chaise in our bedroom. We are working with him to make sure he gets held and snuggled every day. He takes CBD every now and then which helps but you can only give it for about a week at a time until a tolerance is built up then you have to wean them back and start again. We might need to get that kid on some anti-anxiety medication. He has several nicknames including Dobby the House Elf and Lil Baby...no wonder he doesn't have a strong sense of self.

All the dogs weigh between 15 and 20 pounds and are roughly the same size. They have car seats in our cars and we take the pups with us on errands whenever we can. They love riding in the car. When a siren goes off on our drive all the dogs howl along. It's deafening but adorable. We have tons of dog clothes and dog costumes. Yes, they dress up every Halloween. Costumes include a hot dog, cow, taco, ballerina, Chippendale dancer, a bouncer, Yoda and Popeye the Sailor. They have holiday sweaters and even Christmas Eve pajamas. During the winter my husband puts between 3 to 5 of them in a shirt. I personally like to keep them naked...except Walter. He needs the extra warmth of a shirt right now. My husband recently built them a dog park on the side of our house. It even has a fire hydrant for them to take turns peeing on. They LOVE IT.

So that is our family. Life with 5 dogs is really fun but there are days when the only phrases I utter are "who farted?", "stop licking your brother's dick", "why is this wet?" and "WHO FARTED?" In the grand scheme of things, it beats hanging out with humans. Dogs know how to live life. We should all be so lucky.

"Handle every situation like a dog. If you can't eat it or play with it, just pee on it and walk away."
Author Unknown

Dedicated in loving memory of Walter Harper
10/14/1998 to 5/5/2020

Instagram: SherriHarperistheWorst
Facebook: YourWmergencyisShowing
Twitter: SherriHarperist
Podcast: Your Emergency is Showing

Chapter 7

Letter to Jimmy John

By Cory Helie

Dear Mr. Johns,

Heck, I'd say after all the time your sandwiches and I have spent together, I can call you by your first name . . .

Dear Mr. Jimmy,

My name is Cory Helie and dang it, I love your sandwiches. I love the gobs of mayo, Esquire magazine perfect tomatoes, fresh bread, sick veggies and meats, MEATS, MEATS!!! Boy, your sandies are dandy. I'd like to compliment you, because when someone like yourself masters the execution of a fine sandwich as well as a delivery that is both freaky and fast, I take off my hat.

You sir, fucking did it.

On top of my adulation for your sandwiching, I also admire the big game hunting you're known to do. Sharks, Elephants, Leopards . . . Bravo! Those beasts have to be delicious. Now I'd try to hunt them myself, but I lack the planning skills to go so far away and travel home with hundreds of pounds of meat from, say, Africa. Man, you rule.

I think we should all teach our kids to hunt just like you. Hunting large animals is just thrifty and smart. Who wouldn't want to take home as much meat as you can for one single kill? I imagine, it's way easier to butcher one GIANT animal, than it is to skin and butcher 1,000 tiny animals. Which is why God didn't make rhinoceroses the size of squirrels, right Jimmy?

So I would also like to extend my hand out to your bloody hand and shake it, over how gnarly it is that you have taken down so many big game animals.

Now, I'm not just writing to you to kiss your sweet white ass over what you've done, I'm writing to you because I think you still have great accomplishments ahead of you.

One in particular.

There is a species of elephant you may not know about, but it's important that you be the first on record to BIG. GAME. HUNT. it.

The elephant I speak of is the elusive ORANGE ELEPHANT.

The Orange Elephant is large, orange skinned, often already looks like it's been dead for weeks, has a sexy wife, mocks the developmentally disabled, is historically racist, was good in the 90's film 'Little Rascals,' doesn't ask for consent and has a shrimp dick.

Where to find this Orange Elephant? Well, as tough as it may be to track down and kill, it has a physical address which is easy to find . . .

1600 Pennsylvania Ave.
Washington D.C. 20500

It's a big house, ya can't miss it.

Now this orange elephant can be spotted trying to golf, trying to play tennis, ruining a country, not getting hard anymore, and tooting it's own horn in public addresses on facebook. That may seem like it'd be an easy way to hunt this beast, but it is surrounded by a service of secret men and women protecting it. So you'll have to be very sneaky. Maybe get some freaky fast tips from your delivery drivers on this one.

How beautiful would it be to have the head of the orange elephant over your desk at Jimmy John's headquarters? You'll get so much ass from being the guy with the head of the only orange elephant in existence. So much ass.

A J.J. Gargantuan amount of ass.

So that is my challenge to you, sir. Be the biggest big game hunter who has ever walked this earth and take down The Orange Elephant. You got this.

Good luck and I'll see you in the papers.

Sincerely, your dude
Cory Helie

P.S.

And please, if you have a chance to pose naked with the dead carcass of the ORANGE ELEPHANT, that would be super cool. Please use the hashtag #FreeSmells

Twitter: CoryHelie

Chapter 8

Thoughts Can Run, but They Cannot Hide

By Haley Drizcoll

For awhile now I've been trying to figure out how to explain the idea of thoughts themselves having no hiding place. It's a Buddhist teaching that Chyogyam Trunga and Pema Chodron speak really well on. Although our thoughts can stay for awhile, sometimes a very VERY long while, and seem very real and overpowering, there's no place where they can actually stay that's real and tangible, unless of course you write them down and/or memorize them and scream them at strangers like me & my friends. But I'm talking about the actual thoughts (which are technically invisible) that are streaming through our brains everyday and every night. Now, there are obviously different levels of consciousness and awareness of your thoughts. There are thoughts that are more obvious and then there are types of thinking that are much more subtle, like our core negative beliefs, which are linked up with heavy emotions and other distorted thoughts and related memories. But being able to recognize when your ego identifies with any of these fleeting thoughts is key to getting a bigger idea of the observer observing the self (or your higher consciousness being aware of your conscious mind). Identifying ego grasping allows you to step outside yourself enough to get a depth of perspective that you wouldn't have had before. We can so easily associate our identity with our thoughts without taking the time to consider where they came from and why they keep trying to hide from the flashlight light of our higher consciousness.

That's a lot of what the goal feels like in meditation, being able to be with youself and your thoughts, but not attaching to or identifying with or judging any particular thought. Meditation can be really difficult at first, it's like looking at yourself in a fucked-up neglected mirror, and generally a lot of restlessness comes to the surface in the beginning since we haven't developed a lot of patience for being with ourselves. We're confronted by a lot of thoughts we've been low-key been letting control our lives and the disillusionment can really shake up your ego. But as you practice patience with yourself it will become easier to see and redirect certain types of thinking that don't benefit you or others anymore. Eventually through the practice of simply being with yourself for as long as you can, you will develop enough compassion for yourself that you'll be able to lovingly make mindful changes to the narrative of your story, the story being how your life plays out. And what's past that, according to most zen and buddhist practitioners, is absolute emptiness. Absolute emptiness is awareness before you or I or we or any of the dualistic discursive thoughts that our egos are constantly trying to identify with and take us away from our true nature. This level of awareness if where thoughts cannot hide. That's emptiness & that's how you tap into your natural unlimited resource of basic goodness, which does not need the ego to survive. Connecting with this emptiness is how you can take the power back from your ego, which is constantly creating new delusions and confrontations resulting in confusion, delusion and eventually suffering. We're all just different manifestations of this emptiness having an awareness of itself being aware of itself, trying our best to get back to that basic goodness and essentially connect with the Universe again. And that emptiness is always there, although our dualistic minds may not see it through our flood of chronic thinking. But in this emptiness we are all the same, we are undivided awareness, unbothered by personal or general phenomena created by the causes & conditions of living in a world designed for cyclical suffering. We all have the ability to pause our thinking and rest in this emptiness, which is your consciousness in it's purest form. It is so much easier (and bearable) to see your own delusions and the ways you're deceiving yourself and others when your mind can rest in a neutral place with no judgement. Our minds can be a huge source of deception for ourselves and others if we don't take mindful pauses to fully be with ourselves. So you had better slow down if you want to actually observe the changes and get to know yourself! If you're here and you can it's worth a shot!!

Twitter and Instagram: HaleyDrizcoll
Website: soundcloud.com/judgedrizz

Chapter 9

Time Vassal

By Cody Ullrich

I used to have a bit of a drinking problem. I think anybody that has blacked out more than once has an embarrassing story to tell. Maybe you've thrown up in a houseplant. Maybe you've called an ex and cried on their voicemail only to realize you actually called your boss. Maybe you were eighty-sixed at your favorite bar. Maybe... you blacked out, climbed into an Uber, and woke up the next day in the middle ages.

I couldn't remember everything that happened the night before. When I came to, I found myself waking in a haypile in the middle of a town filled with stone buildings. Men and women wandered through the village pointing and smiling at most things they gazed upon. Children played about with swords that looked to be made of foam. I could see in the distance, a jester was smoking a cigarette. Some walked past holding what appeared to be plastic cups containing what I can only assume was meade. Many were dressed in garb that was not quite fitting for the era, but I was aware historians could be wrong from time to time. I knew I was in the middle ages.

As I gained my wits, a woman in a corset stood over me with her nostrils flared. "Ugh, you smell awful. I appreciate committing to your character, but come on, dude," she said unto me.

Startled, I sat up and ran through the crowd into the treeline and did not stop until I could no longer make out the castle from whence I fled. I stopped in a grove and sat upon a rock to catch my breath and think through the mess in which I found myself. Doing my best to recollect events from the night before, I recalled speaking with a friend about some kind of festival he recommended, but I could not remember what type of festival it was. At some point, I responsibly climbed into an Uber. I could not say with any certainty where I requested the driver take me. It was, however, clear to me that this was no ordinary Uber, as it ultimately transported me into medieval times.

At first, I found myself depressed in the situation. It's just as my ex girlfriend said, I thought, I will spend the rest of my life living in the past. This depression was soon overtaken by my realization that I must find a way to survive in this time.

The first thing I did was throw my phone away. I did not want to be caught with what would certainly be seen as a box of witchcraft in the middle ages. I wanted to avoid burning at the stake at all costs.

I built myself a hovel out of sticks. It was a humble hovel and hardly stopped even the lightest rain, but it was my hovel and I was proud of what I built. At night, I would sneak back into the castle to steal food. Oddly, the castle was completely cleared out each evening after roughly nine o'clock. I assumed they were a superstitious people and avoided the dark for fear of something otherworldly. Using this to my advantage, I pilfered what I could. I found mostly typical medieval foods- giant turkey legs, steak on a stick, and of course, Dippin' Dots. This allowed me to survive as I returned to my hovel before daybreak.

As time passed, I knew I had to move forth and establish myself in this world. I thought long and hard of a way to make my mark, then a brilliant idea crossed my mind. I don't know why the thought hadn't hit me earlier- nobody has written Stairway to Heaven yet! It could be me, I could be the one! Certainly, I would be worshipped as a god in this time, were I the man who penned such a ballad. My problems would be few.

One evening during my nightly pilfering, I stole a lute and took to the woods. From memory, I recalled the notes of Jimmy Page and the words of Robert Plant and eventually transposed my own passable version of the tune. I was prepared to march into the castle and impress these simple villagers.

In preparation for my first trip into the castle by daylight, I mastered the tongue of the era, mimicking speech patterns I remembered from media like Game of Thrones, or side characters in the classic film, Black Knight, starring Martin Lawrence, for I was much like Lawrence in my situation and I would be wise to learn from his mistakes.

I paraded into town, lute in tow, proudly singing my tune. There's a lady who knows- I was a sweet little minstrel. ...All that glitters is gold- I began garnering attention. And she's buying a stairway to heaven- I had them in the palm of my hand. A gallant knight approached, lifting his visor to speak.

"Hell yeah, is that Stairway to Heaven? Right on, man!" he spaketh.

How did he know? It baffled me for a short while, then it hit me. It was in that moment, I learned a horrible truth. Of course, how could I be so foolish and how did it take me so long to figure it out?

Someone else travelled back in time and wrote Stairway to Heaven before me?

I had to know who it was. I was not alone, someone else climbed into a time traveling uber in a similar manner and found themselves here with the same thoughts and plans to plagiarize Led Zeppelin. No one could be trusted.

I retreated again to the woods and found my hovel in disarray. It may have been because it was poorly constructed and not built to withstand the elements, but I knew the truth. My time-travelling rival had discovered he was not alone and this was his doing. He destroyed my hovel to send a message. This meant war.

I found myself ill equipped for self defense, let alone to engage in potentially deadly combat with such an adversary, and decided to enter the town and seek a blacksmith. I entered a shop and was greeted by a gentleman who offered to sell me his wares. He showed me a mighty claymore and spoke of its benefits.

"This would make a great decoration for the mantle if ya wanna get this sweet claymore right here," he said in an oddly anachronistic accent, of which I was suspicious.

"Where did you say these weapons were created?" I asked.

"In my garage," he responded.

Migaraj, I thought, Migaraj is not a kingdom I have heard of. For some reason, I decided to trust him.

"Very well, my Migaraji friend," I said. "I am not looking for a weapon to hang above the mantle, I would like something that will provide me with a means of self defense."

He looked at me perplexed. "Self defense? I mean, I suppose you could get yerself a bo staff, but if you're looking for self defense, why not just use a firearm?" Clearly this man had mistaken me.

"You have me wrong, good sir. I am no mage, and I am not able to set my arms ablaze, so I must find another option besides firearms. I will take the melee weapon you have recommended."

I was pleased to find that this shopkeeper was willing to accept modern currency and less pleased to find the cost of a bo staff in medieval times roughly matched what one would expect with 21st century inflation. I had few options and decided to pay him for his wares.

While about, I realized my clothes were not fitting to the era and it was important that I make a deeper effort to blend in. I visited a tailor and was shown a cache of hand sewn garments. This weaver also accepted modern cash and requested egregious amounts of it to fit me into what was essentially peasant's garb. It was very fitting to the era, and were these modern times, I would have commended her for her dedication in recreating such a costume, but these were obviously not modern times, so I reluctantly paid for the clothing.

As I trekked through the village, a stunning maiden caught my eye. I was stricken by her figure, her face was pale as if she seldom left home but to pretend to live in a fantasy world, and her hair flowed in brilliant hues of green and purple. I grabbed a nearby nave that appeared to be familiar with her and asked her name.

"Oh, what? You mean that chick over there?" he elegantly spukenth.

He then told me her name. One that would ring through my head and heart as they should through the valleys of yore into the millenia to come. A name fitting of such a beauty - Brittany.

As I gazed upon her, a woman approached. She saw my garb and must have thought me a servant, approaching me as one would a gentleman who mistakenly wore a red-collared shirt into a Target. She looked at me with her bobbed haircut, seeking information.

"Excuse me, where is the Water Wench Show and what time does it start?" she spakuntheth unto me.

"I know not of these water wenches and I ask that you leave me at once," I replied.

"That's no way to speak to a guest, let me speak to your manager!" she retorted.

Oh no, I thought, she seeks to speak to my lord, of whom I am not fully acquainted. This will leave an awful first impression upon him. Worse yet, what if she sends an angry raven's letter to the king and I am beheaded for insolence to nobility? This is too much attention.

Pressure mounted as she started a scene and I did what I had to. I struck her with my bo staff. The village people screamed and chanted for my undoing.

"Woah, that guy should be charged with assault!" they said.

I waited for the king's guard to arrive and escort me to my fate, but they never arrived. Instead, two uniformed officers from the Douglas County Police Department apprehended me and took me to the local jailhouse.

In those dark moments I realized I did not travel back in time that fateful night. No, I blacked out and requested the Uber driver take me to the nearest Renaissance Festival. They delivered me to my destination and now I am awaiting trial for my misdeeds in what I thought was a very bygone era.

Website: CodyUlrichComedy.com

Chapter 10

WEEDEALER303

By James Draper

I was walking around Whole Foods, as usual, with my phone in my hand. My phone was always in my hand. It had to be. I was hungover of course, but I was happy. I had just gotten out of a long term relationship and somehow I felt pretty good. I was experiencing an unusual surge of confidence that I had never felt before and I was sure it wasn't going to last.

I looked at my phone because I have to look at my phone. I was grocery shopping for other people because that was my job. It was easy, I was good at it and I hated it. I fulfilled customers order's through an app, so I was always on my phone. I saw every notification immediately. I had just gotten a text from my ex. It was an angry message and she called me a coward. That was devastating. I thought we were friends. What had I done to piss her off? God I am such an asshole. Did I do something to hurt her? I didn't want to hurt her. I really hope I didn't. I probably did. I am a piece of shit.

So I went to the first register and fed some register tape through the printer, tore off the paper and wrote down: "I am a piece of shit and I don't deserve love or happiness." I folded it up and put it into my back pocket so I could read it frequently, which I did, and it was pretty helpful. It helped remind me that I am a piece of shit.

I was feeling despondent and was sulking through the aisles, but then I remembered that there was a party that night. The thought made me feel better and offered a slight glimmer of hope. Spirits downed, then spirits up. So much for the confidence streak. I don't have a problem.

After work I went to an early comedy show downtown at my favorite bar. I sang karaoke and drank 2 high lifes, and when my song was over I left for the party. I stopped at a liquor store and bought two 24oz cans of cheap beer and a double shot of Jim Beam. Six drinks should have been enough for the night, but the problem was that at the party there were liquor bottles everywhere, so I grabbed some when I finished my stash and started sipping. I couldn't control myself. I opened them up and they opened me up. I was good at this. My friend Nelson taught me how to drink when I was 19. Take a swig from a mixer, pull the bottle, and another swig from the mixer. Repeat. My confidence started growing again, so I imagine I must have come off as pretty charming and witty, but I honestly don't remember because everything was pretty hazy at that point.

With my memory starting to fade, I decided that it was time to head home. I walked outside and unlocked my bike from a street sign and set the lock on my handlebars and rode home. I don't really remember the ride home that night but the good thing about home is that you can always find your way back even during a blackout.

The next morning I woke up and it was very late. At least it felt late. I couldn't tell because I couldn't find my phone. Where the fuck is my phone?! I was hungover, of course. I opened my laptop to confirm the time and I was right. It was 2pm. I needed to find my goddamn phone.

I checked Facebook to see if anybody had messaged me. Maybe somebody had my phone. Apparently I had sent a Facebook message to a woman I hadn't seen in about seven years. It was creepy and inappropriate and I don't remember sending it. Then I noticed I posted a Facebook status using a racial slur, and everybody was asking me if I was okay. How did I get that drunk last night? But then I figured it out. Somebody stole my fucking phone.

I immediately googled "Where's my phone" and its exact location popped up. I don't remember signing up for this service, but it was helpful and privacy is dead, I guess. I must've dropped my phone on the ride home. It was raining that night, so maybe it was for the best that it was recovered. I was tired and dehydrated and hadn't eaten yet, but I had to have my phone. Everything else could wait. It would be a long bike ride up north.

Luckily, my roommate walked in and offered me a ride right

before I was going to leave. I climbed into his Volvo and we drove to the exact house where my phone was located. As we walked up to the house my heart was racing, and I was glad to have backup. I approached the door and it was wide open. I could see everything inside through a screen door. There were like six sketchy looking dudes inside, and one of them was already in the doorway, so I muttered out, "Excuse me sir, but did you guys recently find a phone?" "Naw man, no phone here," the guy in the doorway said, but then a young kid walked up to the door and said, "Don't even lie man, it's right here," and handed me my phone back. 2% battery left. I didn't want to say thank you so I just turned around and walked back to the car.

Now I could start worrying about other things. We drove through Burger King because I was barely hanging on at this point and needed to eat, but for some reason it was closed. Impossible. So we headed back home and I ordered food from the Chinese place across the street which I've never liked, but I had to eat something right away. I tried to call in an order but my phone was not working. I investigated and found the sim card missing. Fuck. They took that too. So I walked down to the restaurant and placed an order and walked back up to my apartment. I got my laptop back out and tried to search for a T-Mobile store. They were all closed except for the one in the mall which was open for another hour. Now it was time for damage control.

Whoever found my phone must've had a good time, because they made several racist, homophobic, and misogynistic comments to my friends over some of my social media profiles. Luckily, some of my friends came to my defense saying these comments were out of character for me, but I still had to go through all of my history to see who had been messaged and apologize to everyone for things I did not do.

For a lack of a name, let's refer to this phone thief as Wee Dealer, because he tried to link his account to my phone, and now I had access to login from a weedealer303, which is funny, because there is only one 'D', which makes it look like wee dealer. Wee's emails were mostly playstation store receipts, and dishwashing job opportunities, and my only advice is if you're trying to find a job, maybe change your email, Wee.

Wee had replied to a tweet using my account to a gay comedian I follow, which was just an innocuous tweet about having a good Pride, with a simple monosyllabic gay slur. The comedian screenshot this and posted it to Facebook and above the caption tagged me and wrote: FUCK JAMES DRAPER. I had to message him and explain what happened and eventually worked it out, and started locking my screen from then on.

Fifteen minutes later, I walked back down to the restaurant and picked up my only meal for the day, and then walked back up to my apartment. After a few cautious attempts I was able to pick through some of the beef and broccoli, but time was quickly running out, so I gave up and biked down to the mall. I locked up my bike and entered the mall. I walked up the stairs to the T-Mobile store and of course there was a long wait. There was only one other person ahead of me but it felt like a never ending line. I was irritable and impatient. My thoughts were scattered and I looked disheveled. I was sweaty and shaking. I have a problem.

It was finally my turn, and with about two minutes to spare, I told the cashier that I needed a new sim card, and he brought me one immediately and without charge. I missed my improv class and I hadn't even had my kombucha yet, but at least I had my phone back. As I was leaving the mall, 'Stay' by Rihanna came on the stereo. I was in the corridor headed toward the exit, and when the haunting piano refrain drifted into the atmosphere I froze, completely paralyzed. The lyrics kicked in and I burst into tears, frozen in place, because it reminded me of karaoke, and the relationship I just lost, and the fact that it was mostly my fault. I knew what would make me feel better, but I felt so sick I could barely eat, so drinking probably wouldn't work either. I finally got home and I admitted to myself that I need to learn how to control my habits.

Later that night I walked to my friend's house to play Donkey Kong Country, and only had one drink instead of eight. It felt good to be in control of myself, even if it was for only one night. Then I smiled when I realized that it was actually okay for me to feel happy, just as long as it wasn't all the time.

Twitter: DraperTweets
Insta: TheRealJamesDraper

Chapter 11

The New Kid

By Mikey Weil

It was June 12th, 1979. Tim's family packed their last box and closed the door to the moving truck. His father just accepted a manufacturing job on the other sideof the country and the family was moving for better opportunities. Tim turned 14 two days before the move and had to say goodbye to all of his childhood friends. It was the worst birthday of his life.

There wasn't much to do in the small town of Pleasant, New Hampshire. Tim's dad went to work during the day while his mom galavanted around town joining every club and social gathering she could. They unpacked and set up the house just as summer was coming to an end. Tim's parents signed him up for sports, but he always ditched practice and games to go do something on his own. It wasn't hard for Tim to hide things from his parents – they barely paid attention in the first place.

Tim was quiet. He wasn't one to go out of his way to make friends, but that was alright with him. One night, he took his bike down a different route and happened upon a cemetery. He hit the brakes hard, almost throwing himself over the handlebars.

The cemetery sat along a hill, shaded by tall willow trees with a single road running through the middle of it. Tim smiled – he had finally found his favorite spot in town. For a kid who loved ghost stories and found the beauty in everything dark and gloomy – this place was perfect.

As he got settled upon the hill, he took out a pen and paper and started sketching his surroundings. Tim dreamed of one day illustrating the comic books he loved reading.

When cars drove by and the headlights covered the cemetery in light, Tim ducked down behind the graves to make sure he wasn't seen. He knew this would be where he would spend most of his days and he didn't want to do anything to jeopardize that.

For the next few weeks, Tim spent every day in the cemetery. He knew this was an unorthodox activity for a kid his age, or really anyone, but that didn't bother him. Tim always made sure he was home for when his dad got back from work, but really wanted to see what the graveyard offered at night.

Late one night, while Tim's dad was passed out in his chair and his mom was out at the country club, Tim snuck out of the house and headed for the graveyard. He was a little scared at first, but the moonlight hitting the graves was one of the most beautiful things he had ever seen. Tim took out his notebook and as soon as the pen hit the paper he was startled by a whisper around the corner. Tim knew he wasn't alone in the cemetery. Was he finally busted by the cops? Was there another loner there like him?

Tim gathered his belongings and ducked behind a tall and wide gravestone. He was soon relieved to realize it was just a group of high schoolers. The five of them came up and greeted Tim. They were over-friendly, as if they didn't want to scare him.

There were five of them and they each had a shitty beer in hand. One of them had a joint in the other and you could tell he took one hit too many.

Over the next few weeks and into the school year, Tim spent almost everyday with his new friends. When they weren't at the cemetery, they could be found cliff diving, chasing trains, or shooting bottles of beverages they demolished the night before. They were loners, but they had each other. In school, kids left Tim and his friends alone. His parents never made an effort to even introduce themselves to Tim's crew.

On July 5th the following year, the gang hit up the cemetery, as per usual. They were always respectful there. They spent their time in the corner, hiding out from any passerby. This day was different though. Tim and his friends watched as a group of cars pulled up outside of the cemetery.

Parents, brothers, sisters, and grandparents came out of their cars carrying flowers, pictures, and keepsakes. Tears were shed, laughs were shared, and memories were reminisced upon. Tim hid behind a few gravestones, trying to avoid any trouble. His friends laughed at him and told him not to worry.

About 30 minutes later, the families all got in their cars and drove away. Tim was curious. He left the group and headed to find out what was drawing all of this attention. He followed the road in the cemetery and came upon five newly decorated gravestones. The date of death on each of them read July 5th, 1978.

Each name, the name of one of his new friends he had made that year. He turned around and his friends were nowhere to be found.

Tim never saw his friends again. He never told anyone about what happened either.

Every year, on July 5th, he would revisit these graves. He eventually became friends with all of the families, but never told them how he really knew their children.

Twitter and Instagram: HottWeils
Website: Driftmouse.com

Chapter 12

Don't I Know You?

By Megan O'Neil

I dedicate this story to Doris Rauh, a family friend. She kindled the fire in our hearts. RIP

The summer before I started high school, my mom was diagnosed with breast cancer. I remember her mammogram appointment because it was right before my soccer practice. Dad was dropping her off before me, and Mom wanted to tell me to fuck off after asking too many questions. It was a fine example of when I've been too smart for my own good.

Me- "What are we doing here?"

Mom- "I have an appointment."

Me- "What kind of appointment?"

Mom- "Just a check-up."

Me- "You don't normally have check-ups here. What kind of check-up is it?"

Mom- "MEGAN SHUT UP! I have a doctor's appointment, okay??"

My dad gave us kids, my two brothers, my sister, and me, the news very bluntly a week later when she wasn't in the house to answer questions. He had us walk away to take it in. We all found couches to soak into and slow all the thoughts that whirled through our heads. I'd be lying if I said I wasn't upset about how this happened, along with the presentation of it all. My parents could have used a PR rep to untangle the mess, but nobody votes for their parents. So why bother being tactful about that sort of thing? I guess?

She had a mastectomy a month later. For the boys at home; that is when the surgeon takes the entire boob, nipple included. She flashed me post-op and it was devastating. A Kevin Hart bit flashed through my head, "She ain't got no nipple!"

During which her brothers and sisters, nieces and nephews, and her husband and kids all went on vacation together. She said it was fine. We would have believed her if she said it wasn't, but off we went and had a time. I'm still very uncomfortable with how that played out, but she milked that guilt for all it was worth.

Mom was sitting pretty at home, with an exact replica of her hair on her head so nobody would have to know about her cancer, but still tried to make me feel bad. Conversation had always been a strategic tool. She knew the importance of presentation. If there was a way to use tone and voice to her advantage, my mom would exploit it. I wasn't feeding her ego, and to egg a response from me, my mom shouted, "Megan, I have cancer! I could die!"

She was an incredible interrogator, but this was a wild, desperate statement that could not belong to the likes of my mother. My mom taught me women have been fighting with their words since Jane Austen. Yea, she could die. I could die, too. We could both die in a car accident if I pulled the steering wheel out of her hands and out of the street. She was yelling at me like she wanted an emotional reaction! Do we start talking about how the inheritance will get passed around the family? Was I supposed to comfort her until she transitioned into the gamble that is an after-life?

My mom used to give me grief for my crying spells. "No more of this, oh-woe-is-me crap!" She'd tell me. Well surprise, surprise, mother, it turned out to be depression all along. This was difficult for her to understand. She was a T-38 instructor pilot that left the Air Force before women were allowed to fly fighter jets. She told us harrowing adventures as a lesser gender overseas on deployments. Now this crazy lady on board was scared of a little cancer? So this was my opportunity to pull her head out of her ass. No more of this, oh-woe-is-me crap!

I had to review with her everything I knew about the situation; it was a small tumor, she picked aggressive treatment options, and I was playing soccer with her doctor's daughter. What's more, she had great healthcare, probably because she had a highly-skilled job, where she could ask for enough money, and then also afford to sign me up on a soccer team with her doctor's daughter. I knew she was going to be fine, and I told her so. It was relishing to humble her with a clubbing of facts.

As I was in college 5 years after this point, she wrote me a letter about our conversation, and said 'it reminded me that I needed to be a mom'. Does that mean she didn't raise me right? Had I not learned enough to understand what I was saying? How do you still find the heroism and overlook the humility? Of course my mom was brave. But I didn't need her to be a mom right then and there. I needed her to get over herself and truly see how much control she had in the situation.

With the latest changes the world is throwing at us, I can imagine the overwhelming, topsy-turvy feel of cancer, or a similar diagnosis, that would force you to not work, change your lifestyle to avoid newly discovered vulnerabilities, and receive highly-sought treatment. Something that no one really wants to talk about either, because it reminds us that the future is uncertain. Everyone else can imagine it now, too.

I just saw it as her getting lost in the fear sauce, when she looked better confident. Maybe in a sense she needed to be a mom, because it was the task in front of her only she was qualified to do, and her way of coping involved getting hyper-invested in our athletics, and harping on our not-good-enough grades. Yes, I was glad she got back to work. She fought cancer and walloped it, as most people would expect from her given circumstances and legacy of resilience.

Admittedly, I outed her cancer diagnosis, but I was subtle and with decent people. I would fix her wig in front of friends at gatherings. She had this synthetic, wiry hair that required patting down into place. You needed to be gentle with the wig, but then the hair was stubborn. I would get caught up in repetitive, targeted pets. It was like my dog at the door when she was locked out of the house. I'd offer to fix my mom's hair during a conversational lull, and she would accept because she couldn't fix it like natural hair, and was too proud to embarrass herself. Then I would be pawing at the side of my mother's head, fervently, until her friend finally decided that maybe I'm not 'just that weird'. Once my mom admitted to her cancer diagnosis, her friend choked up with tears. She had lost a family member to breast cancer, and the love she shared with my mother brought them into a moment of solidarity. Which opening her heart to loved ones did for her.

So, how does this tie back to the title? Well, when my mom's hair started to grow back, it was shockingly curly; curlier than I ever knew her hair to be. It naturally coiled as big as nickels, and grew out of her head instead of down the sides. She had to transition to new hairstyle tools and products, i.e. relaxer mousse, silk du rag, and a pick. Enjoy that picture for a moment. I like to imagine her keeping a cigarette in her mouth while she works her hair with both hands. Not that she smoked, but a girl can dream. The answer to this question, 'Don't I know you?' is no.

This monumental moment took place in Brooklyn's, across the roundabout from the Pepsi Center, a short time after her last chemo treatment. Mom and I were grabbing food before the Nuggets game, finally at a teen-angst cease-fire. It was a mother-daughter bonding event that we could both enjoy after a turbulent beginning of high school and the successful end of her chemotherapy.

The place was packed, as you would expect before a Pepsi Center event. Our personal bubbles had to shrink to accommodate for the limited space, yet butts of passing people rubbed our shoulders. The TVs were tuned to the pregame show at a volume slightly above the customer ruckus. A man approached our table, one not in a wait staff uniform, and so was dutifully ignored. Just another person trying to get through the room. But then he pointed at the back of my mom's head, side-stepped through a narrow opening, and asked her a question the moment he was in view. He spoke confidently and quickly, ready to accept an invitation to sit with us. Something about a group name.

My mom has always had that perfect tone in her voice that balances impatience with grace. It can unsettle those not expecting a quarrel. She used that to ask him to clarify his question. It shook him, as it would anyone. He took the pause to re-evaluate and discover that he thought wrong. Nonetheless he repeated himself, although embarrassed. "Do I know you from temple?"

She furrowed her brow, told him no, and sent him on his way. We exchanged a glance after. My mom's post-chemo hair was the likeness of a Jew-fro, and this public mistaken identity confirmed that. I'm relieved my family wasn't racist for thinking the same thing. Thank you and fuck cancer!

UpRawr Entertainment

Chapter 13

Sex & Gristle

by Meghan DePonceau

Show Me on the Doll
Where you want me to touch you
Because your doll collection is creepy
and if we start having sex
I won't have to look at it

Chat with Singles in your Area, Call Now
I've been Footlocker married
and loved like a dog muzzle.
Just left wondering what brilliant thoughts
ran through the silenced teeth that bit into it.

I've been Walmart cheated on
And loved like a losing lottery scratch off
Once in a while, a homeless man will pick me up
Just to check the math and drop me disappointed.

I've been Applebees' divorced
and loved like the muffler fell off six miles back.
Whenever I hear someone say "I like puzzles"
I glare at them like they are my Rosetta stone
and shout, "run"

Anonymous Sex
Is good, because
when you only sleep around casually,
with strangers,
you don't care what they think
About all of the crumbs on your bed.

All of it on 21
All we did in vegas was die
and I put a bet on our time of death.
I loved everything wrong with you
down to the mold on your dishes.
all we did in vegas was die

Plea from a Lifeboat
The iceberg
Didn't save the Titanic from its own wreckage
So, stop calling the fucking iceberg.

Partners
I looked around at your dinner party guests
Thought to myself, "he hates all these people"
Then our eyes locked
Your smirk, your out of character martini
To match with mine
It was then I knew, you poisoned the wine.

Learning to Compromise
Three different roommates
Three different types of milk in the fridge,
Skim, 2%, whole,
All expired.

Bartender's Oath
I might not respect your choice,
but I will pour what is asked of me,
judgement free, as long as you ask politely

When I Die
I'd like to be pickled, jarred and served
to horrific bar patrons,
as a delicacy.

Pardon the Partition, Peaches
We sat with our backs to the night sky
Drinkin' jugged whiskey off ancient graves
Your hands down my shirt
My hands in the pockets of your enemy
Everything around us dripped & oozed with purpose

We woke in the bed of your truck
Hungover from the binge lying.
Infected & addicted, sex turned to needles
We desired to be stabbed together in permanence

After our love was immortalized in ink, you begged for my hand.
This merger and acquisition led to full blown inquisition.

Paperwork, it's come down to paperwork
Courthouse marriage,
Motel consummation,
Drive-through divorce?
You don't get to marry her
In the place you broke my heart.
I ain't signing shit.

Reunion
The hotel charged my credit card,
for your who knows what kind of fuck fuck fuckery
Your lack of conscience
& superb photographic memory
Has me on the telephone
With a desk clerk somewhere in Canada.
And I'm not even mad
I just vomit up predictably, "How'd he look?"

Twitter and Instagram: MeghanIsAJoke

Chapter 14

More Dopamine Please!

By Christina Kleemann

The year was 1984. My parents had relocated from North Dakota, where my Dad was born and raised, to Nashville, Tennessee, where I had been violently pushed, out of my mother's body. My mom wanted to be a country singer, but there was one little problem: she cannot hold a tune for anything. We then moved to Livermore, California for a while. My parents had friends out there. My older sister, who was born in California, was 11 when I made my debut. In 1986, my family moved back to North Dakota. Fargo was where my other sister was born. Five years later, came my brother.

I grew up in Bismarck, ND. When I was five years old, I was "diagnosed" with Attention Deficit Disorder and was placed on Ritalin. I have always been a naturally hyper person that had a hard time focusing, so for that, they gave me a magic pill. I spent a majority of my childhood feeling like...a science experiment. "Something is wrong with her." "She is broken, but we cannot figure out what is wrong." I attended Northridge Elementary School in Bismarck from first to sixth grade, which I am pretty sure is standard. Around the age of 11 or 12, my parents figured out that Ritalin came with so many horrible, unhealthy side effects, so in their journey to figure out how to enhance my concentration, they started putting me on various vitamin packets. When that did not work, back on Ritalin I went. To be honest, I had many temper tantrums and "outbursts," because I simply did not know how to deal with myself. I have always been a melodramatic person ever since I was a little girl. Having an intense and passionate personality is something I grew into.

When I was in 6h grade, my teacher and "learning disabled assistants," grew scared of the fact that I was not eating. I simply had no appetite, which was a side effect of the 20 milligrams of neurological stimulant my brain had been under for quite a few years at this point. These "academic morons," clearly had no clue as to the laundry list of side effects that come from a strong methylphenidate. I had been on 20 milligrams of Ritalin, and during either my fifth or sixth year of Elementary school, the school system figured I was still "too hyper," and recommended to my mother that I go on 30 milligrams of medication. My mother and I were sitting in the typical white, uncomfortable, jail-like doctor's office that I had so frequently been to. My mother told Dr. Jeff Smith, my childhood doctor, "the school wants Christina on a higher dosage of Ritalin." Dr. Smith informed my mom "that if I give her a higher dosage, it'll fry her brain, and I am not willing to do that." I remember those words from his mouth, like it was yesterday. This is a memory I have never forgotten. I mean...let's be honest, if I had millions of dollars in my bank account, pulled a Charlie Sheen and taken drugs voluntarily, doesn't that sound like more of a fun life anyway!? DUH! Winning!

My parents got divorced in 2000. This was a very painful time for not only myself, but also my siblings. Please do not misunderstand, I had a plethora of wonderful childhood memories. I also had many painful ones, and who would I be, if I was dishonest about the experiences I have had? To the reader, I enjoy using quotes, to accentuate my sarcasm. I moved to Colorado, to live with my aunt and uncle when I was 17. I had to escape the dysfunction of reality. My Uncle Dan, the person married to my mother's sister, witnessed how I was being treated by the school system in Bismarck. That I was perceived as "different." "I had a learning disability." "I'd never amount to anything, and I'd have to be okay with a mediocre life because greatness was out of my reach." I would like to thank God, for giving me a dopamine deficiency, and any other chemical swimming through my brain, that is low. I firmly believe that many people have chemical imbalances, and either are unaware of it, or may not know how to treat it. It is my sincere hope, that mental health continues to be a typic that is addressed, and not to be feared or shamed. For so long, I was afraid to feel broken. I could not acknowledge that something "felt off." When I moved to Colorado, I spent quite a few months feeling upset with my parents for the Ritalin. How could they not know the side effects?" But, what if they truly through they were doing what was best? Sometimes people truly do not know any better.

I lied quite a bit in my past. I never did this to intentionally be malicious. I lied mostly to friends because I was trying to fill a void in my life. I wanted things to seem greater than they actually were, mainly because I did not realize the power of "just being yourself." So, with guys that I romantically fell for in the past, I formed a very strong, quick and rather unhealthy attachment with them. I went on to create this unrealistic, perfect-life scenario in my head and then when things circumstances unfolded differently, I felt a strong and deeply rooted sense of rejection. That inner rejection triggered my childhood messages of "See, you're NOT good enough." "You don't deserve happiness!" "You're not worthy." For me, this is a project that I am currently vigorously working on. I am truly learning that perspective is everything. Instead of having hatred and anger in my heart, I am learning the art of forgiveness, which seems to come in a variety of colors and paint styles. Since I am "slightly" emotionally messed up, this is what I would imagine the inner narrative of any guy who meets me, to be:

"Roses are red, violets are blue, bitch, you're crazy, but you're also kind of cool!"

To divorce myself from my intense side for just a moment, I want to acknowledge that I have also always had a fun, goofy and sarcastic personality. I did not always know that I was funny. This is certainly not a talent I would have ever discovered in my 20's. I needed an outlet to escape from the crazy mentality I had wrapped myself in for so long. I did not start comedy until I was 33. For me, comedy represented bringing out my vulnerability. Letting of my ego, pain and taking the audience on a journey of pain, discovery, laughter and relatability. It takes incredible nerve to get on stage and perform, but I pride myself, especially now, in taking my nerves and using them in a creative and positive way. I needed laughter. I was tired of hurting myself and not doing anything constructive with my thoughts. Comedy to me, is bringing the truth to a difficult situation. Being able to laugh and relate to painful and positive things. To me, I have met so many incredible people in the Denver Comedy scene that have transcended into best friends and confidants. Speaking from an existential perspective...perhaps our individual journeys are supposed to serve as a guide in helping others. Try not to fixate on the pain and just realize the perspective(s) you can gain from every situation. Live your life and laugh as many times as you can. Doing a set at an open mic is a lot like life in general: you have positive and negative experiences...it can make you nervous as hell...and while it really is all about the timing, ultimately, all you can hope for, is a memorable connection with your audience, and a feel-good chemical reaction...known as dopamine.

Instagram: Christina_Kleeman_Comedy
Twitter: C_Kleemann

Chapter 15

Does Feminism Belong in Stand-Up Comedy?

By Bridget Callahan

Hi! How's everyone doing tonight?

I'm good, I'm good. I'm so happy to be here tonight with you sexy folks. Give it up for the eight other guy comics on the show tonight! And give it up for your host who brought me up here by slightly suggesting a speculative consent scenario with my ass!

You know, my parents hate me for not marrying rich, but that's nothing new.

My mom's all like "How are you supposed to take care of us in our old age on just your barista salary? What did you go to college for?"

And I'm all like, "Look, I'm sorry I can't buy into the colonial narrative of being possessed by some rich white guy who secretly collects live butterflies in boxes and gets his rocks off watching them knock themselves out against the lid, but that's a fairy tale for girls who can afford pedicures. And anyway why don't you take care of yourself with all that money you made destroying our generation with bank fees and corporate tax loopholes? College is a goddamn lie."

Did you know you don't have to love your parents? It's true. They have to pay your phone bill regardless.

I'd like to get paid as much as the guys I work with, but the guys, they don't think that's fair because everyone knows the only reason I still have a job is I smile and am nice to customers. And you know, they *could* smile and be nice to customers too, but if they did that, who would get the actual work of scowling and complaining about shit done?

Anyway, it's hard to smile when their massive amounts of talent and intelligence are clearly being wasted in this job no self-respecting man should be forced to do. So really, they're working harder just keeping it together against the indignity of it all. Whereas everyone knows I actually like being nice to people 'cause it's natural for me. Why should I get paid as much for something that's easier for me? If anyone deserves a raise, it's them.

Every time I light my own cigarette, I think about becoming an arsonist.

I do smoke weed. Who here smokes weed? (Pause for applause.)

I think weed should be legal.

For girls, not for guys.

Because when girls get high, they do cool things like: write stuff, go to clean water rallies, pet our animals a lot, listen to music without borrowing judgmental attitudes from the 90s.

Guys get high and just play video games, in-between screaming about super-hero movies and arguing that Twitter represents the whole world, and therefore the Democratic Socialists of America are going to win every house seat next year. Sometimes they get high and go do something exercisey, so they have something to talk about for the next month. Then they start a podcast.

I started a podcast once. It was about the tv show Riverdale and Redefining Intellectual Standards for Media Consumption, it was called Fuck You, I Like Riverdale.

Isn't abortion great? I love abortion. If it weren't for abortion, I'd probably be stuck in Piedmont, Ohio, married to some roofing salesman I don't know, and writing a mommy blog about making my own almond milk.

But thanks to abortion, I can choose to follow my dreams, even if those dreams mean being a penniless wanna-be artist who spends her life going on a series of ever escalating and terrifying Tinder dates with divorced roofing salesmen.

I bet the Republicans would be all about abortion if we made it legal for credit cards to give out "You've Been Pre-Approved!"

letters in the waiting room right after. Feeling a little down because you just went through an out-patient procedure that cost you a shitload of money and you don't know how you're going to pay rent? Here, have a $500 limit. Go get one of those craft cocktails we know you love so much because we convinced you to feel Instagram shame. Feel that shame, girls. Break out your hipster witch hats and oversized sunglasses and get some Rise filters on that skin, ladies, fucking glow it up, make some bread, masturbate with succulents, raise a cattle dog who loves wearing bandanas and sniffing pussy. Be ironically lank, as if your bones have all turned to soft shark cartilage, sink into your skeleton. Look mildly ashamed to be caught looking pretty. Now hug it out with one of those protesters outside the clinic, because Love is the Answer and also money and also never telling anyone you had an abortion.

I love cocktails. I also love adderall. I have no idea how I would live up to the complex expectations of The Woman who Has an Amazing Career But is Also a Perfect Girlfriend with a Perfect House, Yoga Thighs, and a Creative Nonfiction Essay in the Atlantic without adderall.

But man, the first shit you take after being on adderall is sooo hard. Like, rock hard. I imagine it's like giving birth to a baby, only the baby's name is Well, Actually, and it's made of glass ceiling bits. It's almost erotic, trying to push it out, and you think man, maybe I should have listened to Kyle, had another five drinks, and tried anal. Kyle and I met on Tinder before I learned to never swipe right on any pictures that have a microphone in them. That's Kyle over there. Hi, Kyle!

Kyle is going to get up here and tell a dated joke about Hillary being raped in prison by al-Qaeda operatives. The same one he's been telling since his first open mic 6 months ago, which was still three years after Hillary stopped being relevant. It's what we at the club here like to call "time to have a cigarette and pretend for twelve minutes that cigarettes don't kill you and America isn't a dying pro-lapsed shithole of toxic masculinity." Every other comic will be out there already, because they don't stay to listen to the women, which I think we can all understand.

Recently, people have been asking if feminism really belongs in stand-up. So political. This isn't philosophy class. Makes it so other people feel like they have to watch what they say or that woman is gonna tell all her knitting friends you're sexist. And god, all they ever talk about is dating.

I'll make you guys a deal- I'll stop talking about what it's like to be an angry woman who's been subjected to the manipulations of weak, sensitive baby men since she was 15 on AOL chat if y'all each get up here and publicly state for the record that you would never open for Bill Cosby or Louis C.K. or that one guy Jill accused of groping her when she was sleep, but y'all are still FB friends because he runs a couple shitty $30 for 15 min shows, and after all Jill didn't tell anyone else except some other girls.

Alright, there's the light. I'd like to finish this out with a poem from Andrea Gibson...

A previous version of this piece was published originally in The Tusk.

Twitter: BridgetCallahan
Instagram: SharpShinyClaws

Chapter 16

Jesus, That's Weird

By Sara B Sirius

It can still be an interesting story if it doesn't happen to you, right? Because none of the exciting stuff that happened in this story happened to me.

While scrolling through Facebook on a Sunday afternoon I see that I have an unexpected connection to a recent stabbing spree. Considering we've had two mass shootings in the past few years (including the multiple-fatality stand-off at the Planned Parenthood offices up on the mesa) it was still big news in a mid-sized city like ours.

This particular incident took place the previous Friday night. A crazed knife-wielding scuzzball wearing a blanket like a cape took off on a rampage around 1:30 a.m. starting at a 7-11 on 8th Street. He followed a bike path on foot that took him through a homeless camp where Fountain Creek and I-25 run parallel and are crossed with a major east-west artery forming a web-work of bridges and ramps, with some parts still under construction. It all ended about an hour after it started and a mile away downtown. In the course of it all, several people were wounded, some seriously, before he was finally tackled by local citizens and apprehended. Luckily, no one died.

Ghostly footage of the perpetrator caught by a surveillance camera mere minutes before he was finally stopped made it onto Facebook, showing him walking boldly up a sidewalk heading north, pulling his blanket tighter around his shoulders. He'd left a half a dozen victims bleeding in his wake by then.

And what was my connection? An acquaintance of mine posted that when her ex was leaving a bar at closing time with a friend Friday night they were confronted by the man. The psycho was asking people if they believed in Jesus before coming at them with his knife. The two dudes, victims 7 and 8 of the spree, were able to pin the aggressor down and hold him until police arrived.

Wow, I think to myself. I am not a big fan of the guy that I know. He's an alcoholic jerk who in the past dated and abused my daughter for a couple years after leaving my Facebook acquaintance; geez, what a soap opera. Now it's all water under the bridge that I torched. He and I are not on speaking terms. But yay, he was brave, he gets to be a hero, good for him.

There's a sweet scintilla of irony that I swear I never wished on him in a million years. He's a prominent artist in town, a painter, and he ended up with defensive wounds on his hands requiring stitches. There's a sweet scintilla of irony that I swear I never wished on him in a million years. He's a prominent artist in town, a painter, and he ended up with defensive wounds on his hands requiring stitches. No permanent damage is expected but he'll be slowed down for a while. Maybe now he understands better, you do what you gotta do to survive.

When Tuesday afternoon rolls around I bundle up and hop on my bike and ride to a weekly comedy open mic on the west-side. My route takes me through the bridge area with the homeless camp where mostly men are hunkered down in blankets and dirty down coats, their meager possessions stacked around bikes and bike trailers and shopping carts, or piled under holey tarps. There but for the grace of God go I. Still, I never slow down. I pedal through too fast to be asked for cigarettes or change.

Arriving early to the open mic, I perch at the bar and order a beer. I end up sitting next to a short, stocky fella who reminds me of a bull dog with his barrel chest and buzz-cut flat-top. He's wearing a crisp plaid western shirt, blue jeans and cowboy boots. There's a beer and a shot in front of him. He exudes the aura of a man who has no time or patience for people who sense auras. Nevertheless, prompted by a poster on the wall I open with a joke.

"You know, you might have a drinking problem when the Jägermeister stag is your Patronus."

Two comedy rules pop into my head instantly when he doesn't get the reference: if you have to explain your joke it isn't funny, and gauge your crowd.

We move to safer topics. I'd never seen him in here before. He says he's from out of town but living in a nearby motel while he works with a road crew. It's not his favorite job but it pays good money so here he is after work, checking out this bar for the first time. I tell him I'll be doing stand-up in a bit and he shrugs, buys me a beer and lets me know he probably won't be sticking around for that. I appreciate the candor since it came with a free beer.

We chin-wag about past jobs, our kids, and the record player behind the bar spinning oldies. He circles back to his job to tell me about something weird that happened the week before. They were doing ramp-work down by the freeway. A man wandered into their work zone acting sketchy, asking them if they believed in Jesus. He got agitated and pulled out a knife, brandishing it at them.

"I wanted to take him down. I could've." His eyes were steely mad. I didn't doubt him in the least. "But we have protocols we were trained in so if we wanted to keep our job we had to call the police. A state trooper showed up, talked the guy down, and sent him on his way without confiscating the knife or anything. That was a mistake because that guy ended up stabbing a lot of people later that night."

"Dude! I know the guy who tackled him and held him down until the cops showed up. Now I can say I know someone who was there at the beginning of the spree and at the very end!"

True to his word my drinking buddy left shortly before the show started. Whatever.

The next morning I was up and at it, heading to a food bank. I am not very well off and I'm not ashamed to say that it helps to get a little help sometimes, you know?

It was a brisk, gorgeous ride, blue sky and high clouds, snow on the mountain tops in the distance and sparkly frost on the ground. People are already at the church when I get there, some in a line and some lucky enough to be waiting in their scrapheap cars. I get my number and join the queue. A lanky dude blows warmth into his cupped hands and wonders if we'll get any snow.

"It's cold enough," I reply, "but I don't follow the weather like I should so I can't really tell ya." You never know when the low heavy clouds will start rolling in over the peaks, cloaking the mountains before dumping a load. It's late January and there's plenty of winter left.

We chat a bit and the man tells me that he hopes it doesn't snow so he can make it to the hospital to visit his friend. Our breath is punctuated with tiny fogs which I secretly pretend are word balloons for my own personal entertainment.
"Oh, what happened?" I ask.

"I was hanging out with him the other night in his tent and he was complaining that he didn't feel too good. He figured it was his liver problems acting up and he might have to go see a doctor. He drinks a lot."

He kinda laughs and pauses to blow on his hands again before shoving them into his armpits.

"About twenty minutes after I left, this freak came through the camp asking people if they believed in Jesus and he pulled out a knife. Got my friend and a couple others before he left and ended up stabbing more people downtown."

Gesturing with index finger and thumb, he concludes, "I missed all the excitement by that much."

"Jesus," I said. "That's weird."

Email: sbsirius@aol.com

Chapter 17
Bible Picture Book: W/O Pictures
By Colton Dowling

Authors' Inspiration: Growing up, I was indoctrinated in evangelical Christianity. Obviously, many questions I had about the Bible went unanswered. Hopefully, this chapter can answer some of that young person's questions. These are really stories taken from the Bible, if you do not know anything of the bible, these are my favorite parts.

Narrator: I think we should start this with a montage, an ice breaker if you will...Here are three quick and fun shots.

SEEN:

In the 1st scene you see Jesus healing a paralyzed man by telling him to stand.

In the 2nd scene you see Jesus 'cleansing' a leper by touching his head (the leper's).

In the 3rd scene you see Jesus helping a blindman to see - by spitting in his eyes. Mark 8:23

See that? Pretty Good

Narrator: It's important to note that anything a God does cannot be a miracle because a God can do anything: that's er'y day for an all powerful God. To solve world hunger He shouldn't feed people, if He was any good at His job, He would eliminate the need to eat. To solve for humanities' sins, He decided to replicate himself as a Jewish mage...That's where our story begins: Jesus has a lot of God's powers and he can perform any act with the slightest touch, yet sometimes he does...touch...Remember when Jesus met his 'best' friend Peter?

SEEN:

> 1st picture: Jesus and Peter are both walking on water, while making intense eye contact (Peter is shirtless and has a tight perm).

> 2nd picture: Jesus is still standing on the water with his hands on his hips. Peter is treading water. Jesus has a speech bubble that says, "I told you to look me in the eye's Peter..." You can see Peter has a smirk on his face, a smirk that suggests he knows that him and Jesus are about to grow so close together. *Mathew 14:22*

See that? Pretty Good

Narrator: You see, Jesus only had to make eye contact with Peter to help him walk on water. He actually did not even have to make eye contact. Remember when Jesus turned all that fish and bread into more fish and bread? Why didn't any of that crowd bring lunch?

SEEN:

1st picture: A Jim Halpert (from the Office) looking man in business attire, talking to a 'Pam' (from the Office) in pantsuit, "I thought they were providing lunch at this seminar"

2nd picture: Jesus yelling at the top of his lungs to 5000 people, "I'm God, making miracles. Everyone gets a fish." Jesus was hitting it big time, he was Oprah of the Jews, "You get a fish, you get a fish, you all get fish!"

Narrator: They weren't cooked fish, you think they had baskets and baskets of cooked fish?? No that was raw fucking fish. And just eating a raw fish? The fuck.

3rd picture: Business woman eating a raw fish sandwich (pita bread wrapped around a rainbow trout - no condiments) *Mathew 14:13*

                                                See that? Pretty Good

Narrator: Ok yea, they had bread too. So they all had a raw fish sandwich, everyone. No condiments. All just to listen to this guy yell at everyone about how marketplaces shouldn't be centralized.

Narrator (continued): I mean those fucking fish, they showed up with how many fish? Ok why didn't anybody bring a sack lunch? That's a miracle?? Listen, I was waiting tables one time. One cook. And a 20 top walked in the door. It was a fucking miracle that I fed them all. What did they get? Oh raw fish sandwiches. They didn't get a fucking choice, they were lucky to eat at all. Miracle.

Narrator: Hey! Sorry. Back. I took a quick talking break, but now I'm back, it might not have been a long time in your experience, but it was seven years in my time. It's not that time doesn't exist for me, it's that we aren't on the same scale. Did you know that Jesus was a convervative? Which meant that he actually prescribed to the Persian style of marketplace (opposed to a Greek/Roman centralized market). On the way to protesting his modern day Walmart he performed the miracle of yelling at a tree.

Seen:

> 1st picture: Jesus holding a barren tree trunk and barely whispering death threats. Mark 11:12

See that? Pretty Good

Narrator: Seriously, one of my fav' verses: Mark 11:12-16
> *"Jesus was hungry. Seeing in the distance a fig tree in leaf, he went to find out if it had any fruit. When he reached it, he found nothing but leaves, <u>because it was not the season for figs.</u> Then he said to the tree, "May no one ever eat fruit from you again." And his disciples heard him say it. On reaching Jerusalem,*

Jesus entered the temple courts and began driving out those who were buying and selling there."

Narrator (cont.): Sure the miracle of Jesus yelling at a specific fig tree that was not bearing fruit, out of season is a good use of magic...but then he and his friends went to the Bazaar and fucked shit up...for a miracle.

Seen:

> 1st picture: Jesus and crew kicking over, like 20 tables at a bazaar (themed to the music, OMC - How Bizarre...time doesn't exist) Matthew 21:12-17, Mark 11:15-19, and Luke 19:45-48

See that? Pretty Good

Narrator: Naturally, the miracle of kicking over a bunch of small business owners tables is a fun miracle - but sometimes a miracle will come to Jesus. When Jesus got some traction, he went on that conference circuit and was giving another speech (no prompter) in a packed out house (literally). Side story: a group of friends, decided that the most "crippled" one of them, should see Jesus. Rising Action: they brought him to the house where Jesus was talking. Conflict: The thing is, that house was packed with people and they couldn't get in. Climax: They did the only thing that they could do...hoist him up to the roof, DIG a hole in the roof, and lower him down in front of Jesus.

Seen:

1st Picture: Jesus talking to a packed out room, while a hog-tied-man is being lowered from a hole in the roof

2nd Picture: Without touching anyone, Jesus cures all paralysis in the hog-tied-man

3rd Picture: To the side of Jesus, the owner of the house stands, thought bubble, "finish the miracle by fixing the fucking hole in my roof" Mark 2:1

See that? Pretty Good

Jesus never did finish that miracle. And it rained that very night and ruined his new red Persian rug. That owner never really did get rid of that miljewy smell...

Narrator: Remember when Jesus spit in that blind man's eyes?? Why did Jesus not just say "See?" rather than spit in his eyes? Lolol Jesus was bad at his job.

P.S.
God is a woman, yeah. God is a woman yeah. Yeah when we're said and done...and tbh I'm happy about that because if God was a man...heaven would be a man cave and smell like farts, beans dip, and beer. *Open-Micer 1am*
P.P.S.
I know the difference between 'seen' and 'scene' you fucking troll.

Can you handle?: @ColtonDowling, @biblepicturebook

Chapter 18

My Precious

by Laura Thompson

Silently cursing last night's revelry, Caroline sat in the lecture hall dreading the onset of a killer headache. She had rushed out of the hotel this morning, but managed to pull off the outward appearance of a put together executive. On the inside, she was still a mess. Thankful for the complimentary pastry and juice, she nibbled on the corners of a strawberry danish while the presenter continued her pre-packaged inspirational speech. "Inspiration my ass," Caroline thought. She desperately struggled to stay awake while the petite, perky, superwoman in front of her excitedly described her third trek up Mount Everest. "Good for you, lady," Caroline thought, as she slowly sipped her cranberry juice. "Good for you." She ached for the addition of the tiniest bit of vodka to slow the impending hangover.

Caroline let her mind wander to her upcoming plans. She was headed to Brooklyn that afternoon and couldn't wait for the vacation she sneakily managed to tack on to the tailend of a work conference. "Listen," she muttered under her breath, "you want to send me to Philly, you sure as fuck better believe I'm headed to New York to party before I head home." Luckily, she had some friends in the Bronx and she was looking forward to hitting them up to cop some weed. Yes, a blunt and a floppy slice of pizza, followed by sushi and an ice-cold, extra dirty martini was exactly the evening she craved. That is, if she was ever released from the hell of this seemingly endless lecture.

All of a sudden, Caroline was wrenched from her daydreams by one chilling thought - she had left it behind, her prized possession. The only thing since the divorce that was hers and hers alone. The one thing that brought her reassurance in the midst of the end of a marriage and the beginning of a new life. How could she have been so careless??? She always, ALWAYS checked her hotel room one final time before checking out!!! "Well," Caroline thought, "the only thing I can do is call and hope to God it's still there... Fuck. Me." As the overly-coiffed mini-powerhouse of a woman continued to speak, Caroline started tapping her foot in angst. She held her breath and used every bit of her mind to will the woman to, "Just. Stop. Talking!" Finally, like magic it happened. The room erupted in applause while Caroline bolted for the door almost sarcastically clapping and cheering. She wanted the room to at least think she was engaged.

It didn't take long for the front desk associate to answer her call. "Hello," Caroline responded nervously, flushing and quickly looking left to right to ensure no one was listening. "This is Caroline Moore," she whispered, covering her mouth over the phone. "I stayed in room 458 last night? Uh-huh, yeah, it was a lovely stay, everything was perfect. Anyway, I'm pretty sure I forgot to empty the drawer next to my bed and I checked out this morning. Could you please ask housekeeping to check for me?" Caroline paused and crossed her fingers. She nodded to the conference attendees walking by. "Hold on, let me check," the concierge politely said, putting Caroline on hold. The insipid hold music did nothing to place Caroline at ease and she watched the seconds tick by before the woman returned to the line. At this point, the concierge's tone had shifted from polite and cheery to dripping with disdain. "Ms. Moore?" she said. "Yes?" Caroline reliped breathlessly, the telltale rouge of embarrassment returning to her cheeks. "We have your belongings at the front desk. You can pick up your, err, items, at the front desk this afternoon."

Soon, town cars arrived to usher conference attendees to the airport or, in Caroline's case, the train station. She slipped into the luxury leather-clad interior of her town car, but could not relax. She had one other companion for the long car ride: a middle-aged, white, balding investment banker. Needless to say, he didn't even acknowledge Caroline as she took her seat. During the ride they sat in silence; him, reading the Wall Street Journal, her, watching the blur of the city through the rain-splattered window. As the car approached the hotel, Caroline murmured to the driver that she would just be a moment. The impatient look on the banker's face made her seethe, but she collected herself and entered the hotel lobby. After all, she was on a rescue mission.

Caroline marched to the front desk and introduced herself. An introduction was not needed. "Hello. I'm Caroline Moore. I called earlier about the items I left in room 458 last night?" She saw the knowing look the front desk employees exchanged and felt her cheeks begin to inflame for the third time that morning. "Yes, Ms. Moore. We have them." The concierge wrinkled her face in revulsion as she handed Caroline a small white plastic bathroom trash bag, it's opaque surface hiding it's contents. Caroline grabbed the bag, whispered a word of thanks, and ran back to the car. For the next hour, she could think of nothing but getting to the train station to open the bag and make sure everything was accounted for; she sure as hell was not opening it in front of her impatient backseat neighbor. After an eternity of a commute, Caroline arrived at the train station. She yelled a quick thanks to the driver, grabbed her suitcase and the bag, and rushed into the station. She didn't care about checking the departure schedule for her train. Her only mission at this time was to find it, her most precious possession: her everything - her vibrator.

Now at this point, one might wonder, "What was so special about this vibrator? Why on earth is this woman making such a big deal about a sex toy? Couldn't she just replace it?" Well dear reader, this was no ordinary, run of the mill, battery operated, mass produced, piece of trash. No. THIS was a $180, plug into the wall, make you cry tears of joy, full-blown, powerhouse of a vibrating wand. Thanks to this amazing piece of machinery, Caroline had been able to secure more orgasms than a hooker on speed. No human could match it.

She rushed into the train station and sat on a bench with a crazed look in her eye. Others gave her a wide berth as she tore through the white plastic bag, muttering "Where is it, where is it???" The bag finally ripped, out tumbling its' contents: a half eaten bag of gummy bears, a few tissues, some mints, a phone charger, a wrinkled copy of Cosmo, and finally, FINALLY the pink and white piece of mechanical engineering brilliance that she loved so dearly. "My precious," she whispered, Golem-voiced, as she clutched the wand to her chest, tears streaming down her face. "My precious."

Caroline spent the next several years in and out of relationships, but no matter who she dated the one constant through it all was her friend, her lover, her confidante - her vibrator. They traveled together, they enjoyed weekends at home together, and sometimes, they made other people come together. One day, after years of service, the vibrator's motor finally wore out and came to a slow, agonizing, grinding, stop. Caroline realized it was gone, truly gone, but this time she wasn't sad. When she left her vibrator in Philly, she learned the most important lesson of her life, one that stuck with her for many years. It took a vibrator, of all things, to teach her that the old adage was true. "If you love something, set it free... If it comes back to you, it was meant to be."

UpRawr Entertainment
Instagram: FemmeandFunny
Twitter: Poz2Vent

Chapter 19

Baseball & Me

By Brad Galli

You probably think baseball is boring. Some of the questions you may ask are: Why are the games so long? Why does it move so slow? Why are some of the players fat? I get it. You think baseball sucks. I don't.

I've loved baseball as long as I can remember. My first memory as a kid is from April 9, 1993. I was three years old. I remember the date, because it was the date the Rockies played their first home game in team history at the beautiful old Mile High Stadium. My dad and three of my uncles were going to the game and they didn't buy me a ticket. I don't blame them. I was a huge pain in the ass at the time and I probably wouldn't have watched much of the game. My dad and uncles wouldn't have been able to drink as much as they did either if they had a child with them, and when you are at a Rockies game you've got to pound those Coors Lights baby.

The memories in my mind from that day are shockingly crisp. I remember driving in the car with my parents from my home in Pueblo, CO to my uncle's house on the Southend of Denver. My dad drove and my mom sat in the front seat. I was strapped into a car seat in the back and I was excited and I didn't really quite know why. All I knew about that day was that baseball was involved and I wanted to be a part of it. I didn't know who the Rockies were. They were a brand new team. At three years old I don't think I knew any of the teams in the Major Leagues. All I knew about baseball is that my dad and I would play it in our front yard and that it was glorious.

We got to my uncle's house that day and I went and played with my cousins Chris and Mike for a little bit. I lost track of time and then I noticed that my dad wasn't there anymore. I went to my mom and asked,

"Where did daddy go?"

"He went to the game with Jeff, Mark and Chuck," she said.

I was fucking devastated. "How could my father not take me to the game?" I thought. What kind of piece of shit doesn't take his three year old son to a baseball game? I felt betrayed but I probably got over it in 20 minutes. I was three and would forget things almost immediately. Kind of like a dog. Also, I was a whiny like any three year old would be. I had a great father who worked his ass off and just wanted to spend a beautiful Spring afternoon drinking a few cold ones while enjoying the ball game. He deserved it and didn't need an annoying three year old wrecking his vibe. My dad also ended up taking me to probably 60 or 70 Rockies games throughout my childhood -- including the 1998 All Star Game. That's a lot of baseball. I was a lucky kid to say the least. I may have been lucky, but the Colorado Rockies were anything but.

The Colorado Rockies fucking stink. Since becoming a team in 1993 they have made the playoffs only five times, they have had only eight winning seasons, and they have never won a division title. The most memorable year in Rockies baseball was 2007. The Rockies won 21 out of 22 games in September and October to reach the World Series for the first and only time in team history. They were promptly swept in four games by the formidable Boston Red Sox in that World Series. 2007 was magical, but aside from a Wild Card Game victory against the Chicago Cubs in 2018 - it is really all us Rockies fans have had to cheer about for the last 13 years.

Despite how dismal of a ball club my Rockies are -- I love them with all of my heart. To be honest, the fact that they are such shit may make me love them that much more. Life isn't perfect. Shocker. Life more times than not disappoints you. Life will get your hopes so high only to stab you in the heart with a dull knife. That's life and that is also the Colorado Rockies.
Being in quarantine has only made me love my Rockies that much more because I now realize what I love about them most -- they are always there. Like clockwork, when the calendar switches to April I know that my boys at 20th & Blake will be there and that they'll be doing their best. They will keep doing their best for six months and then come early October, unless they are in the playoffs (they won't be) they'll go into hibernation

for the winter. It will be a needed break and I won't be sad because I know they will be back in April.

There are 162 games in a Major League Baseball season. Yes, you heard that right. 162. This is another huge reason why a lot of people don't like baseball. I can admit that 162 is an overwhelming amount of games. It is virtually impossible that a fan can come close to watching 162 full baseball games. I don't watch all 162 Rockies games every year -- but I come damn close to at least watching several innings of every game I can catch on television, in addition to the 20 or so I attend in person. I love that there are so many games, because that means that I can rely on baseball being there almost everyday for me. How many people get something in their life that they know will be there everyday for them? I am lucky to have three: My family, my lovely girlfriend, and of course the Colorado Rockies. I'm blessed as the kids say.

Baseball was not here this April though and at first I handled it pretty well. I obviously could grasp that there were more dire issues going on in the world at the moment, and the suspension of a baseball season ranked pretty low on a list of things that really mattered. It was brutal though, and as the days have turned to weeks I only miss it more everyday. I miss the crisp nights at Coors Field in the Spring and Autumn, and the blistering afternoons in July. I miss the inning-ending double plays. I miss the way Nolan Arenado fields a routine ground ball before firing it to first base. I miss checking my phone at work to see that the Rockies are getting massacred by the Dodgers and it's only the third inning. I even miss Bryan Shaw blowing a three run lead in the 7th Inning. More than anything, I just miss it being there. That's it. It was always there and now it's not.

It is a popular opinion amongst many people that sports aren't important. I agree with that one hundred percent. Sports are not life or death. Sports do not discover life-saving vaccines. Sports do not work tirelessly to get innocent people out of jail. Professional sports are grown men who get paid very handsomely to do something that kids are supposed to be doing. That may be grossly oversimplifying, but that is essentially what it is. There are dozens of sports shows on cable and the internet filled with analysts that talk ad nauseum about athletes and the games they play the same way that pundits on CNN, MSNBC, and FOX talk about politics. None of what these sports analysts talk about is that important, but that isn't the point. Sports best function is that it is a release.

Baseball is my release. I have mild depression, and some definite anger issues. Sorry for taking this piece in a dark direction but that is just the truth. Luckily, I have an amazing girlfriend that I mentioned earlier, and I am fortunate enough to be able to perform stand up comedy any night of the week I want in a city as great as Denver, CO. Sometimes I even get paid to do it. I also have a job that wears me down at times, and I have a tendency to get overwhelmed by the mundaneness that life brings. I feel helpless and like there is nothing to look forward to, even though I have plenty of positive things in my life. The feelings are real though, and in between April and October, if I ever start to feel that way I can always look to the Colorado Rockies for some grounding.

I am not advocating that people (especially men) should ignore their problems and just be consumed by the distraction that sports bring but I will say that sports can help. The Colorado Rockies are always there in the Spring and Summer for me. That's comforting. They're usually not very good, but that isn't important. They are there and that's all that I need. That's why baseball is better than other sports to me. It's daily. You can always count on it, and in life -- especially times as uncertain as these, it is nice to have things to count on.

Twitter: BradicalGalli

Chapter 20

Kids Say the Darndest Things

by Brian Kinney

My sister has kept track of the funny things her grandson says. Ah, the innocence of a 5 year old! I originally wanted to submit them in cartoon form, but written word was the final vote. To protect the young, I will refer to him as Bart.

1.Seeing his grandmother bring him a glass of water: "Actually, that has a booger in it."

2. "I wasn't lying, I was kidding!"

3. "Can you smell my armpits? Can I smell yours? Can I smell your feet?"

4. "I know where sweet potatoes live. It's in the ground."

5. Pointing to brown spots on banana: "Did you know that is oxidation? I love oxidation!"

6. Grandma: "Aren't these flowers pretty?" Bart: "Yes, so I want to crush them."

7. To grandma, who is resting: "Do you still need quiet?"

8. Grandma: "Your mom's out at a nice restaurant." Bart: "Do they have gum?"

9. "Are you older than a giant?"

10. Grandma: "Your grilled cheese is ready." Bart: "Are you sure you know how to make grilled cheese? You don't know how to make chicken nuggets."

11. Trying to sleep: "Anybody? Anybody? Anybody in this house?"

12. Bart and friend punching and stomping on stuffed animals:

"We're teaching them how to fight."

13. Grandma: "Doesn't this room look clean?" Bart: "I like dirty. I like my dirty room."

14. "When do I go to college?"

15. "My tummy says I want soda. I'll share it."

16: Grandma: "Who is your favorite Disney character?" Bart: "All of them. Except the princesses. I don't like them."

17. "I don't need anything here but I super want to buy something here."

18. "My brain has a headache."

19: Grandma: "You're God's creature" Bart: "Wait, I'm a creature?!?"

20. "How do you spell E I E I O?"

21. "Mommy put gasoline on my chapped lips."

22. "We must play in these (Christmas) lights , for Heaven's sake!'

23. Watching Frosty, wondering about pipe: "Why does Frosty have a hammer in his mouth?"

24. Bart: "Tomorrow is Christmas Eve!" Grandma: "Actually, Christmas Eve is 2 more days." Bart's lips quiver. Grandma: "Are you going to be okay?" Bart: "You're wrong. You're all wrong."

25. "I drank blood. Well, it was juice blood. It was juice that had vitamins in it, and blood."

26. Cleaning his room: "YOU'RE NO FUN!!"

27. "I'm part coyote and part person."

28. "How do trees know when to stop growing?"

29. "I KNOW ABOUT MY ATTITUDE!!"

30: Grandma: "Let's clean your room." Bart: "Okay, I'll watch you."

31. In a cowboy outfit: "I'm going to arrest you...After you make me a sandwich."

32. "My room's clean...April Fool's!"

33. "Do you guys want me to teach you how to make that farting sound?"

34. "I didn't know that question was in your mouth."

35. Bart: "I want you to buy me a Lego set!" Grandma: "I want you to stop asking me to buy you a Lego set." Bart: "Okay, I'll stop asking, and THEN will you buy me a Lego set?"

36. "I think I woke up too early today."

37. Riding scooter through a puddle: "I'm getting a tire wash."

38. "My nose is clogged with boogers."

39. Bart: "Is 9th grade the last?" Grandma: "No, 12th is." Bart: "(gasp!) I'm not even in first! What grade are you in?"

40. "The milk tastes bad. Maybe they forgot to clean it after it came out of the cow."

41. "When Jesus was hanging on the cross, why wasn't he wearing a helmet?"

42. "These fruit snacks have a juicy part that splatters in your mouth."

43. Bart: "Can I have $30?" Grandma: "No." Bart: "Please?!?" Grandma: "What do you want it for? The ice cream truck?" Bart: "Yeah." Grandma: "How about $5?" Bart: "Okay!"

44. Grandma: "I hope your day turns around." Bart: "My day's

84

not turning around."

45. "Skiing is importanter than school."

46. "When the tooth fairy leaves money, does he or she wake you up accidentally?"

47. Grandma: "Can you say please?" Bart: "I'm saying please in my head."

48. "I concur. Do you know what concur means?"

49. As I'm driving him home from school: "You drive better than Mommy."

50. Grandma: "I'm pushing bananas." Bart: "Pushing's bad manners."

51. Bart: "I bet your blood has lines in it." Uncle Brian: "Huh?" Bart: "Because you're old." Uncle Brian: "Oh, like wrinkles?" Bart: "Yup!"

52. "Were you born in the old days?"

Chapter 21

Deshelled

By Steve Vanderploeg

Though they never really talked about it, the boys knew it was going to be their last summer together. Senior year was only a few months away, and they knew it was going to be nearly impossible not to drift apart, especially considering it has already begun.

Bradley, the glue of the friendship, was likely to receive a full scholarship to Stanford, as long as he kept his grades up for his final year of school. Despite a few fights over love interests, he managed to stay close friends with Dakota, who was planning on going to trade school. They had met at a Bowl-a-thon in middle school which had been organized by local churches, but when Dakota's father passed away in August 2016, the grievances and pain led to both young adults losing their faith together. Then there was Zen, the alpha of the group. Zen was by far the most popular. His parents had a more hands-off, holistic approach to parenting, which allowed him to get in and out of a lot of troubled situations with relatively low consequence. Zen wasn't evil, though he would be the closest thing to the Devil's advocate Dakota and Bradley had met throughout their adolescence.

With only a few weeks of summer left before their senior year began, all three boys had been desperate to have an extra adventurous night. They sat in Dakota's driveway, ignoring the extravagant pastel sunset, complaining that they had wasted more of the season than they had anticipated, while passing around a white glass pipe filled with cheap marijuana.

"Man, I still can't believe Julie cock-blocked me like that. I spent two months trying to fuck Ashleigh, finally got her alone in a hammock, and as soon as I started fingering her she ran outside screaming that she was gonna call the cops." Dakota commiserated.

"You're still upset about that?" Bradley replied. "That was the first week of June!"

"Yeah, but still. I was so close to hitting that fine ass!"

Zen interrupted: "Fuck Julie. Fuck Ashleigh. And fuck this whole town. This place sucks, and if it weren't for you two, I wouldn't even be sticking around to finish up school." Zen cashed out the ashes from the pipe into his hand, only to wipe them on the best pair of cargo shorts that he owned. He grabbed an opaque orange medicine jar, and started re-filling the bowl. "What we really need, is to show this town who's boss! We're seniors now, and we need to let people know that we're ready to be in charge!"

"In charge?!" Bradley retorted, "How can we run this town when only one of us even has a car?"

Zen lit the new bowl of weed, inhaled, handed the pipe to Dakota, and exhaled. Dakota followed the same actions.

"Cars only get you places physically anyways man. We need to go on a mental journey. Something different." Dakota said as the effects of the marijuana started to kick in. He exhaled and handed the pipe left to Bradley.

"Weed is all I need man. I'm not doing anything harder than this." Bradley said. He put the pipe to his mouth, lit the bowl, and didn't inhale. He handed the pipe to Zen.

Zen sat stoned, contemplating in his head while Dakota and Bradley began talking about the Marvel Universe. For about 90 seconds he sat there, not realizing he was starting at the patterns in the concrete without even noticing them. Suddenly, he snapped out of it, "Dakota! I just had a great idea! Do you have any eggs in your fridge?"

"Eggs? For what? You wanna bake a cake at 9:30 on a Thursday night?"

"No!" Zen responded. "I just remembered, I know of this perfect little spot off the highway. There's a cul-de-sac right nearby. We can park there, walk up the path, and have a perfect viewpoint of the highway. When we see a car coming, we throw the eggs, and whoever hits the most cars, wins!"

Dakota and Bradley looked at each other hesitantly, before Dakota spoke up, "I'm not sure that's a good idea man. That could be dangerous and, like, karma is totally a bitch."

Zen shrugged his shoulders.

Bradley, surprisingly intervened enthusiastically, "Actually, that sounds like a ton of fun! Dakota, get whatever eggs you have out of your fridge, don't let your mom see you. We can go to the store and buy a few extra cartons. I'll throw $10 towards it."

Zen spoke up, "Hell yeah! Now we're talking!"

Dakota thought about declining the opportunity to cause mischief with his friends, but instead of speaking, he twisted his body, stood up and jogged inside to his fridge. He opened the door, moved aside a jar of pickles and some cottage cheese and grabbed a carton with 10 eggs. With his head still in the fridge, he paused and contemplated staying home one last time, before he closed the refrigerator door, eggs in hand, and ran back outside to his friends. "Let's go!" He shouted, and they all shuffled into Zen's baby blue 2003 Subaru WRX.

After a short discussion, the three drove slightly out of their way to go to Albertsons, to avoid being recognized at the Kroger their parents all shopped at. They knew that buying 8 cartons of eggs on a dark summer night looked suspicious, but acted as if it were a right of passage as they went through the self checkout lane.

Fully stocked, they got back in Zen's car and drove to the Shady Oaks neighborhood, a community of suburbanites mostly already asleep by this time of night. Without any map, Zen's intuition drove him right to the parking spot he wanted. There were only two houses at the end of this street, and a dirt path that wound around the backyards, running parallel to Highway 6. They walked up it about a quarter mile, cartons in hand, hiking up an uncommonly travelled hill, and suddenly, they had found their perch.

Bradley impatiently grabbed an egg, and tossed it onto the

deserted highway. They heard it crack in a distance and all began laughing. All three began throwing eggs as far as they could, even though it was too dark to see where exactly they were landing. Zen stopped for a second. "Wait! Wait! I see headlights. About a mile down. Let's see who can hit it when it comes." They all paused for about 15 seconds, and when the car was a hundred yards down the road, they all gave their best toss. None came close. They began rationing their eggs for passing cars only.

They sat on the hill tossing Eggland's best for about 20 minutes, getting better and better with their aim. A couple cars swerved out of the way, but for the most part, none of the three were able to coordinate their timing and aim enough to make a difference. With only a few eggs left, a pair of headlights crested over the horizon, heading directly down the middle lane of the road. Zen yelled out "Alright boys. This is our last chance. Let's make it count."

Dakota became suddenly overwhelmed with chills. As Bradley and Zen hocked their last eggs, Dakota hesitated, as if he knew that something terrible was about to happen. As he stood there, Zen grabbed the last egg from his hand, and tossed it aimlessly onto the highway. A red pick-up truck reached the part of the road that was littered with shells and yolks, and suddenly a loud "THUNK."

The egg landed directly on the driver's side of the windshield, and the 2-door pick-up immediately hit the brakes, and began skidding towards the median, stopping just inches before collision. The boys had shocked themselves, and without saying a word, they all began running back down the hill, along the highway, past the two backyards, and down the path to the car.

They ran so fast that as they approached the concrete, they slid, heels first down the sidewalks. Zen stopped. "What the fuck?!" He yelled out. "Who would do this?!" High on adrenaline, it took Dakota and Bradley a second to realize that Zen's Subaru was not how they left it. It was now covered in a strange film, and smeared with shells, whites and yolk. At least 20 eggs totally plastered over the paint and windows of the entire car. Zen lashed out again. "What the fuck is this?! What's wrong with people?" He screamed, right before he noticed a piece of paper under his driver's side windshield wiper soaked in albumen. He pulled it out and it dripped as he opened it up and read it out loud: "Next time we call the cops." All three boys looked up to the most western house, to see a silhouette in the living room window, right before the light shut off.

Instagram and Twitter: SlumDogChillionaire

Chapter 22

I work at a call center and you can too!

(An excerpt from *Cooking for One and Other Things You Can Do Alone*, which is a very *rough* but special draft right now but someday may be a whole entire book!)

By Sarah Benson

If you are reading this book, you probably do or will work at a call center. It's just simple statistics.

I work at a call center but I didn't even realize it until months after I had been hired because the call center where I work is so beautiful and filled with snacks. (Not all call centers are like this.)

The first step in understanding what it's like to work at a call center is simply understanding and accepting the fact that you do work at a call center. This little quiz will help you realize if you really do work at a call center or not.

Do you even work at a call center: the quiz

1.) Do you spend part of your day "on phones"?

- A. Yes, and every ring is like looking down the barrel of a gun.
- B. Yes, and "it's not that bad most of the time" is what I tell myself because I know there are not a lot of jobs right now and I need the money and moving to another department in this company may be an illusion but at least I can dream.
- C. Yes, and it's super fun/chill because I get to spend time on *my* phone and my manager doesn't know about it.

2.) Do you ever think "this is my life. This is the path I've chosen." And get a little bit sad?

- A. Yes.

3.) When someone on the phone is very angry, how do you react?

    A. Skirt the precocious line between having genuine empathy for them and sobbing as quietly as possible.
    B. Let the person tire themselves out while you play solitaire in another window on your computer.
    C. Start looking for other jobs, knowing full well that you'll never quit because you have a beautiful cat that relies on you for survival and you probably won't get fired because your company is not trying to lose anyone with more than 6 months of experience.

If you answered A, B, or C to any of those questions, you work at a call center.

Perks of working in a call center

Although there's a lot that sucks about working at a call center (we're not even going to open that can of worms because it's too sad), there are some good things, too. I'll outline those in this next section.

Headsets

I never even knew how cold my ears were until I got a job where I had to wear headsets 5 out of 8 hours a day. Turns out these little ears get chilly! And nothing warms up them up quicker than a little bit of faux leather and a good amount of stress.

Speaking of stress, my headset and the things I hear in it makes my body so warm that I actually *sweat*. I can work and workout all at once! What a time to be alive.

One of my other favorite things about headphones is the fact that when you're wearing them, people will think that you're busy. Pop them on when you want to play Solitare and look at shower curtains online. It's nice to look busy without having to do anything except keep your ears warm.

The last really fun thing about headsets is that you can use them to pretend that you're actually doing something else. I'll go over some things I like to pretend in the few, fleeting seconds I have before I actually have to go back to looking like I'm doing my job. (Yes I *am* writing this at work! Way to go, you super sleuth you!)

You can be the CIA agent who tells the undercover CIA agent what to say from inside a van parked a little down the road from the sting site! They wear headsets just like yours! No, you're not the "cool" agent who actually gets to go undercover, but you are a really great side character with a little bit of a story-arch. It's implied that you really know your stuff and that's why you have to feed lines to the undercover agent who's hot but kind of an idiot. You resent him but you don't show it.

You can be Brittany Spears in the 90s! Brittany wore a headset just like yours for almost every concert and music video she ever made in her 20s. It was cool back then - so cool that you don't have to even pretend you're Brittany Spears, just pretend you're in the 90s!

Yep, you're in the 90s and you love wearing your headset. You start a trend at your high school and now everyone is wearing a headset and is that hottie finally noticing you? Is he gonna ask you to prom?

He does, and during your Prom King and Queen dance, you realize that he only liked you for your headset. You know who was attracted to you for you? No one yet, but you'll meet plenty of dudes in and after college. Then there will be a bit of a dry spell and now hey, here you are! Living the Dream with your one bedroom apartment and beautiful, loving cat.

You can be an astronaut or a race-car driver! 3, 2, 1, go! In my mind, these professions are pretty similar. Both involve countdowns, going fast and headsets. Wow, clearly you've gotta be a risk-taker to get a job that requires wearing a headset *everyday*. You're brave. What is your star sign? Did you even cry when you were born? Nope, you were probably like "hey world, slap my face on a box of Wheaties because someday I'm gonna get a job with a headset."

You can be a voice actor! I always wanted to be a voice actor and wearing my headset at work makes me feel like I really am one! Because I'm speaking into a microphone and acting like it's completely normal and fine to call tech support before you even try refreshing your screen and seeing if that will fix the problem!!!

Open Floor Plans

A lot of call centers don't even have cubicles anymore because studies show that cubicles make working at a call center worse.

Working in an open floor plan is like being a prairie dog on the vast and open plains but without being able to dig underground. You're just standing on your little prairie dog legs, chewing on grass and running around not knowing what you're accomplishing 100% of the time but looking really busy and focused as you do it. And then the day is done!

I love open floor plans because it's nice to see that everyone else gets yelled at on the phones, too. Also, if you don't fully understand your job (which almost no one does,) you can listen to what other people are saying on the phones and then store those little word-tracks in your brain, and reuse them to customers that you talk to. Understanding context is time-consuming and overrated

Having an income and (hopefully) benefits

One of the great things about living in a country without universal healthcare is that it really makes you appreciate any health benefits you have through work. You suddenly cling to your job like it's an old tire swing and you realize that what you thought was a pond is actually a crater full of nuclear waste.

I know that sounds unhealthy and it probably is! Hopefully you work at a call center that does not make you feel like you're in a negative relationship, but rather makes you feel like you're in a relatively healthy relationship. Like a couple that says they're "too old" to get divorced.

Decorating your space

Here is your chance to use all that creativity you have to stifle for 40 hours a week!

Be it a cubicle, desk, or boundary-less table space that you share with your passive-aggressive table buddy, (although you two are too far away to actually invade each others' space and you kind of wish you were closer so that maybe you could be friends,) you have a little piece of real estate that is all yours in this crazy world. It is technically company property but for these purposes we're going rip a page out of Colonial America's book and say that that desk is yours because you are on it.

Your desk decorations and knick-knacks will non-verbally communicate a lot about you, so you may consider choosing a theme. Themes make people say, "wow, she puts thought into things despite the fact that it seems like the total opposite!" It also makes people think that you are creative, which you are, if you're the kind of person to have a desk theme.

Make sure to pick a desk theme that relaxes you. Also, know that if your taste changes, it's okay to change your desk theme! My bedroom was almost 'skulls and scary psychedelic monsters' themed until I realized that I am actually afraid of most things and that's okay. Now it's filled with pictures of flowers and catoonish bears and has a very "THINGS ARE GOING TO BE OKAY!!!" vibe.

My desk at work is under the sea themed and it calms me down whenever I look at it. I even have a little tiny dolphin figurine holding a sign that says "Life's a Beach!" I still don't know what the artist meant by that. (You know art is good when you don't fully get it.)

The biggest perk: friendships

The friendships you make working at a call center are unlike any other. It's like you're both cows and you can see the slaughter-machine in the distance but you never know when you're going to get there and once you do, instead of dying you just get right back on the conveyor belt. But you have a buddy by your side and they know what you're going through!

You will love your coworkers because you will laugh together and cry together. You will experience emotions with intensity comparable only to that of daytime soaps. You will want to hang out after work, but most of the time you will be too tired from all the hostility and basic math. (Did you know that you forgot how to subtract without a calculator?)

So even though you and your coworkers don't hang out that much after work, they understand because they're also very exhausted from feelings and they forgot how to do math, too. It's a beautiful and tragic wavelength that you're both riding together.

Little whispers

(If anyone from work is reading this, please don't fire me.)

Twitter: SarahMBen
Website: SarahBensonComedy.weebly.com

Chapter 23

Another Day on The Trail

By Gabby Gutierrez-Reed

It is a beautiful day outside, perfect in fact. My girlfriend and I are finally on the hike that we always talked about. We walk up the winding route full of yellow violets and larkspur. Everything is blooming this time of year.

I look over my shoulder, "This is so nice, Rose. I know I say this a lot, but things have been really crazy lately and I want you to know that I will always love you."

Rose smiles, "I love you too, Jess."

In that moment, our eyes connect. Everything in the universe is right.

All of a sudden I see something fly out of the corner of my eye. I look over and a hawk swoops down towards me. I duck and it grabs Rose. She starts lifting up into the air. I can't believe what I'm seeing. A regular sized hawk is lifting my 200 lb girlfriend into the sky. I think quickly and grab her leg. I am pulling with all of my strength, but this damn bird won't budge. Rose is screaming which starts attracting attention from other people on the trail. They start to run over, but by that time my very own feet start lifting into the air. Out of panic, I let go. Sadie floats away, while I feel like I'm drowning. I'm in shock.

I start hyperventilating and pacing. "Quick quick, what do I do?"

I reach for my phone to call 911. A message pops up saying, "Your screen time has gone up 22% from last week." I groan, "Now is not the time, Siri."

I dial and a woman answers. "911, what's your emergency?"

I say, "A hawk just took my girlfriend!"

"Ma'am, state your name please."

"Ugh, it's Jamie Patel. Aren't you hearing me? A living breathing hawk flew away with my girlfriend right in front of me!"

"Ma'am, what's your location?"

I shout, "I'm about halfway up the South Table Mountain Loop in Golden!"

"Okay, ma'am. I'm going to need you to stay calm. I'll have a car dispatched to your location. Full disclosure, this has been happening since the coronavirus outbreak. Strange things have been popping up. There have been reports of talking buffalos and the blue mustang at DIA galloping away with his creepy lil' red eyes. You know, Blucifer." She chuckles. "Crazy ain't it? Anyways, there's not much we can do at the moment because we haven't been able to find the nest where the hawk has been taking people. We've contacted multiple government agencies, but they've had us on hold for two weeks. It may be something that we just have to accept."

My heart is pounding in my chest. "Something we just have to accept?"

The dispatcher continues, "We've deployed a Hawk Task Force with little to no success. We lack the proper experience and training, but the future's looking bright."

Rage starts to boil throughout my body. "How is this helpful?" I scream.

The dispatcher retorts back, "Listen lady! We'd all like to know what to do. We can predict and project all we want, but we still won't know what's going to happen! We can't find the nest alright!"

The dispatcher hangs up. An apple news article pops up on my phone, "Coronavirus straining your relationship? 5 special dates you can have at home." Goddamnit, Siri!

Instagram and Twiter: shishgabab

Chapter 24

Maria

By TC McCracken

Naughty Maria
propelled her shiny new red wheels
up the empty sidewalk
under the black midnight sky.
She summited the park; her eyes squinted
as the full moon reflected upon the undisturbed snow.
The park was desolate
but she trekked forward into the white abyss
with heart, not thought.

There she dismounted
plunged backwards into
Infinite snowflakes.

She sank to the earth
feeling the infinite embrace.

Her body tingled in ecstasy
from head to toe.
Gravity pulled tears of delight
down her cheeks
through her ear channels
to kiss the snow.

Maria's skin and heart glittered
brighter than the moon.

Instinctively,
her arms and legs flew back and forth
caressing
infinite snowflakes.

Her soul painted
a single snow angel.

Away from home
being not naught, nor alone

her lips parted
howling loudly
not at the moon
but howling for
those that embraced her,
Infinite snowflakes.

One by one,
suburban lights turned on
to see the wild creature in the park.

Maria pulled her bare ass up
with her shiny new red walker.
Feet swishing
and tennis balls scratching the cement,
Maria, snuck home
before her daughter would find out.

Laughing
in a state of nature
as air tickled all her skin,
Maria,
thought of infinite things
only possible in a mind
that has been reflecting for 30,660 days.

Suburban onlookers
did not know what to think.
They just saw 2 full moons and 1 angel.

Website: https://mommamccracken.com/
Facebook: https://www.facebook.com/MommaMcCracken/

Chapter 25

How to Start the Best Cult: Netflix Edition

By Nate Earl

We here at Netflix have heard you, America - you just love cults. And what's not to love? Whether you're watching in pity, morbid curiosity, or the smug sense of self-superiority that you would never be so easily swayed we know there's nothing our viewers like more than watching large groups of people having their lives permanently changed by unchecked narcissists. And with the overwhelming response to our docu-series about small, semi-religious institutions like Tiger King, Wild Wild Country, and Goop Lab we are excited to bring you even more of that sweet cult footage you crave.

But we've hit just one snag - we've run out of fun cults! Sure there are the assorted anti-vaxxer or flat earth sects that are running rampant in the country but our market research has shown that viewers find them "depressingly realistic" and "not comforting". So we are putting it to you to find, or even start, our next Netflix Original cult. Below are our guidelines for what we expect in your organization. If your submission is chosen you will receive a $9,500 reward as well as a six-episode miniseries about whatever you want.

What a binge-worthy cult needs:
•A Leader: The key to any good cult is a charismatic narcissist with a plan. While casting for a cult leader may seem like a good idea we recommend finding one in the wild. Anyone with the showmanship and crazed focus of a theater camp counselor will do. We also want the viewers to sympathize with our cult leader, as they will be one of our main characters. Make sure they have an interesting past - perhaps a vlogger or a copywriter for Netflix who is repressed at their job? Someone who would be adored if people only listened to them. He could teach them how to seek the true Godhead...

•A Fun Hook: There have been hundreds of pseudo-religious organizations throughout America - many of which even have video records of their activities. But you don't see them on

Netflix because they never had a fun hook. Whether it's Hollywood weirdos, jungle cats, or activating your serpent-force, all Netflix documentaries need a sexy twist. Now we don't want to retread old territory, so get creative. Perhaps your cult is obsessed with religious nudity or trying to create time travel or even bringing back medicinal bloodletting. If you are thinking of seeking divine truth through hallucinogenic frog sweat that cult is already taken. The right hook has to be sexy and dangerous but not to the point that it offends the viewer. Make sure that your cult's hook can hit all four quadrants.

•Members: Cult members give us a window into how a cult is successfully created. More importantly they allow us to imagine what it would be like to participate in wild orgies or be on a half-year cruise. They worship their divine cult leader and possibly recruit new members (note to self- put Terry on recruitment). It's best if our team can get multiple viewpoints from cult members. The members could have different positions in the cult or different experiences to reflect on in our docu-series. So, if your cult is not large enough to support an inner circle of powerful figures, make sure there's someone in the mix stirring up shit.

•A Problem: Now the story of the cult is great for two or three hour long episodes - but we need to narratively edge the audience for at least eight episodes for a series. So - make sure your cult runs into problems. Do not count legal trouble - our friends at the FBI make that an inevitability. No we mean weird, cult specific problems - an uprising in the ranks, possible in-house sabotage, for example maybe a cult member, let's call them Aiden, keeps getting into the enclosure and licking up all the frog sweat. We have to have something spice up our middle few episodes. Problems again have to be sexy and only kind of dangerous. "Where to hide the bodies?" is a problem that might end the whole series. "How do I get rid of my rival?" can be a through line for multiple episodes and, better, is a problem that many people can relate to. Viewers would never kill their rival but they probably have at least thought about it. If you are attempting to create your own cult we recommend inserting a few troublemakers into your flock if no other problems arise. Though, I can say from personal experience with Netflix cults that troublemakers are drawn to these groups. (Note to self - have Terry kill Aiden).

•Kind of a Mystery: What do we mean by "Kind of a Mystery"? Here's a perfect example: Did Carole Baskin murder her husband? Definitely. But maybe she didn't ;)

The best mystery is something that people can agree on the major points of what happened but still discuss minor details. We want our viewers to feel smart while still having the majority of the clues spoon-fed to them. Just like any police procedural. It must also leave enough room for doubt to not be a complete bummer. The murder of a man is sad but if the man was possibly killed in a freak accident it is a little easier for us as viewers to sympathize with our protagonist, the cult leader. If the cult leader has an alibi, like working overtime at Netflix to put the finishing touches on an ad campaign, even better.

There you have it. We wish you luck in finding America's next top cult! And who knows, you could become a national celebrity, leading your enlightened fanatics into glory. Right after they clean up the frog habitat.

Intstagram and Facebook: UnfunnyOaf
Also, check out his podcast – "Take Care of Yourself!"

Chapter 26

Drop

By Zac Maas

The year: 2321.

The only water remaining: the backwash found in disposed plastic water bottles.

Mountain range: there are no granite faces or arms of pine; these bodies are made entirely of plastic. Millions of bottles, the labels long faded, scuffed.

A fog horn booms, Kurplushhhhh, the pressure release sends thousands of bottles to the heavens; they land with a few bounces before settling. Movement near the eye of the explosion breaks the stillness. A hatch flies open, scattering debris.

A man emerges from the hole and stretches his arms in the moonlight; a hose protrudes out of the pack on his shoulders. He uses this tail to sweep away a large patch of bottles. The hatch is attached to a platform, a porch made of tethered jugs floating atop the ocean of plastic. It moves slightly under his weight, bobbing like a raft. When he bends to put his shoes on his feet, the ventilator on his back shifts--he grunts, stumbling, but retains his balance. The footwear is similar to a snowshoe, with large bottles flattened, layered, and melt welded into boat shapes. It doesn't snow in this high desert, but the ocean of bottles acts like quicksand.

A young girl emerges from the same doorway and fastens a smaller set of plastic canoes to her feet. He leans over and helps her as she struggles to tighten one of the straps.

"You don't want a float to come off when you're atop The Savior, Ivy," Jerimiah chuckles.

Her head whips quickly "Or the only way you'll find me is the smell?" Neither of them had ever actually smelled the surface.

Without air, there is no odor.

"Exactly," he said, patting her on the shoulder. The knocks on her thick plastic armor echoed through the canyon.

Checking the straps one last time he gave the signal to Ivy that it was time to go. He detached their hoses, smiled, held his finger to his lips, and leaped off of the life raft. CRUNCH... CRUnch... crunch... plastic on plastic rang out mixing with the muted hum of billions of bottles quivering in the wind.

Ommmmmmmmmmmmm. He began to sink, but the shoes did their job, stopping him after dropping a few inches.

Ivy had been practicing in the pit since she could walk and rushed to take her very first real step, CRUNCH... CRUnch... crunch....

"It's so loud," she chuckled.

"Come on Ivy; you know better." he shook his head and made a circular motion back to the base.

Did he have to say that she thought, wasn't that just wasting more air? She looked down at the meter on her tank, the oxygen bar bright green--lighting up her mask before her wrist dropped in a sulk. She wasn't supposed to be here, but necessity demanded it. Everything calculated precisely; life here did not have room for choice.

Since the water left, new forms of life had started to grow. Only fungi and bacteria had survived the drought. They were watching Darwin's theory in full swing. This swing, however, wasn't sailing through an oxygen-rich environment (yippee); this new life had learned to harness methane like we use oxygen. The mushrooms unlike us, however, only grew on the tallest peaks.

As they reached the base of a large pile, they began to traverse up, sidestepping, testing their weight. Upon closer inspection, one could see that the plastic formed crude stairs. Jeremiah had floated this trail before. Occasionally, a rogue bottle would break away from the mound and bounce its way down the mountain, clunking into the rim of the eighty foot horns bell. It's blasts were all that kept them from being buried alive.

A few hours in, Ivy found her first mushroom and plucked it with a twist. She eyed it for a moment before shaking it violently. The rain of spores sent off a soft red glow as they reacted with the methane in the air (an aurora sporealis). A gust blew out the candle; the winds started to accelerate.

"This isn't good," Jeremiah said, holding up his hand for Ivy to stop. You're wasting oxygen, she thought as she placed her mushroom into the mesh bag on her side. They were close to the summit, and he picked up his pace, gaining distance on Ivy. It was becoming hard to hear as the bottles turned into wind chimes, the earth's post apocalyptic jug band. Jeremiah reached the summit and his fear was confirmed--off in the distance and moving towards them was a slowly swirling vortex of plastic.

"We need to go. NOW!"

"But... I just..."

"PLASTORNADO," with one last look the vortex began to rise into the air. He bent down and pulled the straps tight on his boats. He moved at a speed that came from years on shaky ground. In one movement, he pulled his knife, cutting Ivy's straps and threw her onto his shoulders... A storm like this killed her mother.

"Hang on," he said as he turned his boats down hill. His shoes were now snub-nosed ski's, and with a pump of the knees, gravity took them. Bottles were shooting into the air with every turn as they carved their way down. The wind was howling, riddled with plastic, the airborne missiles ricocheting off their armor..

Ivy turned her head back; they were now riding down the front of a mountain that was collapsing underneath their skis, the summit falling into nothing, as darkness raced to overtake them.

"We have a collapse!" she yelled over the storm. They had trained for this. "100 meters!," Jeremiah stopped turning at this point and pointed his planks straight downhill, tucking his knees even further. It was hard to see with the air so full of rubbish but Ivy could still make out the abyss gaining on them.

"50 meters!" she screamed. Jeremiah leaned forward even more looking for any advantage he could find aerodynamically. He kept his eyes straight ahead locked on the only light they could see, flashing in front of their home — the lighthouse.

A giant gust ripped out the path before them transforming the incline into a giant cliff. With speed, they hit the lip throwing them into the air. On the wing was the wrong place to be on The Savior. They splashed into the flat at the base of the vanishing mountain sending up a fountain of bottles. The boats did their job and acted like springs popping them to the surface. They had made it down.

About 50 meters separated them from the dock where they had fastened their boats. The splash had stolen all of their momentum, and now Jerimiah moved with Ivy's extra weight in an awkward wobble towards the platform. Stability meant more than speed, because to fall, was to die. Ivy turned her head back once more. The mountain at this point had disappeared, and all they saw was a spinning synthetic blur.

"25 METERS!" she screamed, the nothingness was gaining on them as the bottles behind them fed the storm. The strap on Jeremiah's left boat tore, with nothing to hold onto, the wind took it, leaving him standing there on one foot. With both their weight on one leg they began sinking into the plastic sand.

"GO," he yelled, throwing Ivy off of his shoulders. She hit the dock hard, and began to slip off, her hands paddling for a grip. Her fingers caught one of the hoses, ripping some fingernails from their seat. She pulled herself up, looking back at Jerimiah standing there on one foot, helpless--the blur gaining on him. She grabbed the other nozzle and threw it as hard as she could, warm blood filling her glove, it fell short. The once flat area behind Jeremiah began to drop like water on the edge of a drain.

Standing there on one leg, he did his best to dive to the hose. His fingers grazed the tip, but it wasn't enough. He sank immediately into the plastic right before the plastic itself collapsed into the void. He was gone.

As Ivy stared into the whirlwind, everything began to sink in. She pulled her way to the hatch, and turned to look back. She jumped as Jeremiah shot out of the darkness. His remaining boat caught wind, rocketing him into the air. It was the right place to be. Dangling upside down by one leg, the wind carried him right into her failed rescue; tangling him in the mess, the hose catching securely around his ankle--he became a kite. Ivy pulled, but the wind on his shoe overpowered her.

She yelled at him to cut the straps, but by the way that Jeremiah was dangling limply, she realized he was unconscious or worse. She latched a safety line onto his hose from her suit and shimmied towards him. The wind whipped the line hard almost shaking her, but she held firm inching her way with her ankles locked tight. She could see blood leaking from one of the plastic plates on his suit. When she could reach she removed her knife from her belt and cut into the straps. Three-quarters of the way through, a bottle smashed into her blade sending it into the expanse.

"Fuck" she looked back at the portal and turned back to Jeremiah. "I'm sorry." She began to inch herself back home when the tension of the hose went limp and she began to free fall. A hard jerk sent her smashing into Jeremiah's knee, knocking her unconscious. All that could be seen in the darkness was the red glow of her wrist.

Instagram: MaasComedy
Website: ZacMaas.com

Chapter 27

A Review of About Time

By Joshua Emerson

About Time is a romantic comedy starring Dohmnall Gleeson as 'Tim" and Rachel McAdams as 'Mary.' On Tim's twenty-first birthday, his father, played by Bill Nighy, tells Tim that the men in their family are able to travel through time by going into a dark place and squeezing their fists. They are only able to travel between present day and their birth and only in their own life. It is a campy premise but Bill Nighy's dry, almost sarcastic delivery makes you suspend belief instantly. His condescending attitude makes you scared to ask more about the logistics or the origin of this odd power. It is a crucial scene as it sets up the premise for the whole movie and Bill Nighy is fantastic in it. The next questions are about what have the men in Tim's family used this power for. Money was said to be a foolish endeavor, though it should be noted that Tim's family lives in a Victorian mansion on the coast in Cornwall, so maybe not completely foolish. For Tim's father, it was books, rereading books, talking about books, his job before retirement was teaching literature for a University. And then he turns the question back on Tim. Tim acts as the narrator throughout the movie and in this scene, Tim looks up at his dad and the narrator says, "for me, it was always going to be about love."

About Time has very good pacing through the first third of the movie. The filmmakers give you the time travel premise, make it clear that About Time is about love and then they take you through Tim's first infatuation with someone which he confuses for love, Tim's move to London and then they introduce you to Mary. They are like mini arches of rising conflict and resolved conclusion and the rhythm feels like ocean waves coming in with the tide. And then there is Mary and that is the rest of the movie; the different sagas of Tim and Mary's relationship. And we get introduced to Mary by the end of the first act or twenty-two minutes into the movie.

Mary is played by Rachel McAdams. It is a little odd to see someone like Rachel play somebody mousey, whose insecurity is one of the character's defining characteristics. It mostly works despite how much of a dynamo McAdams is. There is a sweetness and quiet strength that comes through in McAdam's performance.

Because of time travel, we get three meet-cutes between Tim and Marry. On a dodgy night out with Tim's friend, dodgy Jay, Tim meets Mary in a blind cafe. A blind cafe is a restaurant where the meal and discussion take place in complete darkness. As a consequence, our first meet-cute is entirely based on dialogue but the chemistry between Tim and Mary is still obvious. They exchange information and it is clear how excited each character is about finding something new that has promise. Tim has a great line when Mary enters her number in his phone, "I used to think this phone was old and shit but suddenly it has become my most valuable possession." The director uses a shaky cam shot as Tim walks home and it really captures that joy of meeting somebody new that you like. That joy is juxtaposed when Tim gets home by his roommate and landlord, Harry, played by Tom Hollonder.

Harry is a largely miserable playwright whose play was ruined by an actor having a dry. TIm selflessly uses time travel and helps Harry's play succeed but at the cost of losing Mary's number. It feels a little silly, considering how unlikable Harry's character is but it is useful in showing how kind Tim is.

The second meet-cute takes place at a museum, complete with a waiting, musical montage. Throughout the movie, there are these almost mini-music videos. Tim and Mary's interaction is awkward and this is one of the my least favorite parts of the movie.

The third meet-cute is at a house party. This may just be me, but hearing Nelly's Dilemma makes me think about the butterflies I used to feel at middle-school dances. Tim and Mary's chemistry is on display again and the night ends back at Mary's apartment. Even though Mary is mousey and insecure, her straightforwardness about sexuaility is attractive and does not feel forced. She has a good line here when she says to Tim, " I am going into the next room and put on my pajamas and maybe in 30 seconds you can come in and take them off if you want to."

Tim replays the following interaction a few times, which is pretty funny.

Tim and Mary's characters fit each other, they complete each other. Their love is tested twice. The first is by a visit from Mary's parents, with her anxiety for them to like Tim because she loves Tim, is on full display. The second is by Charlotte played by a pre-Wolf-of-Wall-St Margot Robbie.

Charlotte is the subject of Tim's first infatuation when she spends a summer at Tim's family home in Cornwall, which concludes with Charlotte rejecting Tim. But this second, chance meeting, Tim is a more mature man. A dinner turns into a walk home and Tim and Charlotte are at the precipice of Charlotte's apartment and she invites him in. I do not think I need to spend much time on how legitimate of a temptation Margot Robbie is and I am trying very hard to not use the term, "snack." But I saw this movie after seeing Wolf of Wall St and I knew what Margot Robbie looked like naked. Tim makes the right choice and rejects Charlotte and runs home and proposes to Mary.

The wedding scenes are amazing and an orchestra of disaster is bookended by a speech from Tim's father and best man. The movie picks up pace again and TIm and Mary have kids and move into a new home. In this part of the movie, you see the limitations of time travel in its ability to save people from death or from themselves. The score is beautiful and there is this pretty piano piece the filmmakers use throughout the movie as an audio representation of love. It is present from the opening scene and they play with it being subtle and in the background to increasing its volume and having it be this big crescendo.

The movie's message comes out in the last act and it is to live your life with intentionality. It is a good point. I find myself living my life trying to get to these imaginary destinations and I do think I lose something in trying to speed through the parts of my life I deemed transitionary, to my detriment. It is very easy and satisfying to be kind. Spontaneous moments of joy are temporary and they are worth looking for. Overall, I think the movie works very well but there are moments that do not hold up on a rewatching. The score does. The set design feels warm and the performances are good. The side characters are well established and well acted. 7.3 out 10.

Twitter: DangerEmerson
Also Twitter: DeadRoomComedy

Chapter 28

Quar! Quar! What is it Good for?

By Rachel Crowe

Today I did nothing. It was a good day.

Before all this nothing, I used to love donating blood. Not just because my insides were exposed and headed off to unknown adventures. Not only because some part of me would become part of someone else, either. The sweetest detail was that I could be at most 100 feet away from children with leukemia or another annihilating disease I've never seriously considered. I'd be that close to a child who has only ever lived my nightmare and get called a hero for sitting still for twenty minutes. Then, juice and snacks. Then I make another appointment to be so close to death and completely self-involved.

Same for airport security, assuming I show up with enough time. All I have to do is not have plotted the deaths of others in advance and I'll be Fine. Of course, I'm blonde and cherubic so that comfort is absolutely a privilege. It's the naivety to believe the truth is enough to protect me.

My point is that when a situation comes along where you can excel by doing absolutely nothing, grab onto that gold star motherfuckin' tight.

It's okay, then, if my opinions are cock eyed and incorrect. Fine by me.

This horror we're living, it's devastating, seismic - sure- but my world is moving at a pace I understand, Finally. Nothing I want matters. I'm not even near the top of the list. Stooped in humility, I stretch out.

Everything that's left to occupy our hours is lived in the most minute detail. The umbrella broke right before a walk. I threw it out in a trashcan down the trail from our house, not our own dumpster. A careless gesture became an outing.

Returning, I walked through a part of the yard I haven't seen in a while to come in through a gate who hasn't been touched in years. I wanted to remind the gate it is a part of our home.

It's a gentle life I was given. I found a cache of old records. The cat's litter needs more cleaning than it receives. My parent's home is cluttered but never uncomfortable and beckons me with projects. I was always certain the world was off somewhere having all the fun without me, especially when I last lived here. I have proof that's not the case anymore.

I've given in to my personal frothing conspiracy theorists. All the paranoia "The Da Vinci Code" inspired in my pre-pubescent brain blooms. Did you realize the Illuminati only allowed in ecoterrorists with depression? I had no clue. This whole time, the most powerful secret society was being managed by powerful, well medicated and exhausted schemers. I wonder how they vet newcomers. Maybe they set a timer, plop hopefuls down at a pep rally or someone else's family reunion and see how long before they're fully fetal. I always knew the horrible people running the world were evil billionaires, sure. I didn't know those horrible evil billionaires had something in common with me, let alone brain chemistry or that our habitual negligence can kill a cactus.

Now I know they're on my side. They don't care that I exist, but they are helping me. Before quarantine, there wasn't time built in to the work day for laying on the ground. Now there's plenty.

I never thought we could do it. People with depression aren't great at committing to plans. When we do go through with it, it's not usually a net gain for the world. Never thought we'd have the stick-to-itiveness when laying on the rug for a few more hours looked so damn good. We said we wanted a world without underwire and waited for a black hole to roll ourselves into. And oh boy, did we not get the black hole.

Then I peek outside. Lives dissolve into numbers of the dead. There's always more.

The truth of our combined present only truly greets me in foghorn or skywriting (depending on weather) when I leave my comfy cave. She walks in, dumps her bag on the choked kitchen table and I see those colorless blue scrubs. My mother in scrubs is like my mother in glasses- as I know her. Sure, the scrubs are blue and blue is a color. I would put money that I certainly don't have that this shade of blue is a color never seen in nature. Identical scrubs line her closet. It's hilarious and terrifying, like she's living under some fascist rule. My mother's scrubs don't mean lazy Halloween costumes right now.

I remember my mother is out in the world, vulnerable to everything I've only watched. I wonder if the mask-less old woman in line at the liquor store exhaled a germ onto me only to pass on to a new mother whose baby my mother delivers.

Perhaps my carelessness will lead to a woman being unable to hold her newborn for two weeks. Perhaps not.

And then I worry about my father- my delightful, exhausting dad who I rejected those party invitations six and a half weeks ago for. Y'know, like a hero. He has the patience to wipe the what if's off our groceries. I wonder if the hot water I rinsed our apples under was hot enough. Maybe that Fuji is a murder weapon and my unthinking lapse pulls the trigger.

Apparently the cat could be at risk too, although I'm not sure how those First two feline COVID patients contracted it. Then again, cats have barbed penises. They're adorable aliens but I'm not going to understand them.

And then I worry again about my mom. She has a lifelong asphyxiating allergy to most spicy food. I didn't know that extended to black pepper. A few bites into tacos and my mother Flees the table, choking. She's hacking like she'll fall apart. She's so small in the door frame, wearing that unfortunate blue uniform of a soldier. What's the alternate to "Mulan" where a young, healthy woman does, in fact, allow her stooped aged parents to take her place in battle? My mother would kill me for calling her "stooped".

I cry, "I hope you're choking!". It sounds so wrong but I can't stand the other option- that the news seeped in past her mask and bunny suit, past her car I now avoid and into our home.

Those thoughts only Flicker past in rare moments. Mostly, I'm greeted by myself.

Sometimes I welcome myself like a bored dog and my child has come home from school. My tail's wagging. I'm totally over the moon.

Or I wake up at noon and Flop over to glance at myself with pity and understanding. Why muster up shame for ideas of what I should be doing that I never even believed in?

Any time of day and I relax into my own arms, head resting on the shoulder of my friendship. I remember not to be needlessly cruel and never to use that tone with myself. I inch forward, unconcerned if I'm headed anywhere at all.

I'm on a 25th anniversary honeymoon with myself after renewing vows. The sex is comfortable and Filling- Figuratively, literally, all of it. I've missed myself. I never kept secrets from myself until I did. Ignoring myself ate up all of me. Now all I have to do is live well with myself.

As a little girl, I terriFied myself considering how the world might be once I was an unimaginable adult. My generation, we've always been told that now is most likely the end. At the very least, I sleep sure that I can not know what comes next.

As a little girl, I also thought I might grow up to be some American Jane Goodall. I read that the secret to seeing wildlife is to stop looking for them. In silence, animals gather. In silence, the strange miracles of ourselves creep out.

I also learned that athlete's foot wiped out ancient Rome. I won't cite my sources just like you shouldn't double check that. I'm as certain it's untrue as I am sure of the memory. Let's pretend. We're already living in a sick hypothetical- why not? A great civilization upended by stinky feet. Sounds preventable. Now we watch people march off the edge in search of a trim. Distractions costing lives.

Humanity doesn't like to be conquered by Nature. It's

embarrassing and childish. We pretend it's been so long since we answered to a force more powerful and present than a god. We certainly don't appreciate being ambushed by our own mortality because of a whim.

I drink at noon and somewhere else, people die. Beyond a life so small I can Finally comprehend it, the actions of the living ensure their loved ones die.

There are enormous problems outside some front doors, problems that require sacriFice and know-how. My only problem then, and I hope the same is true for many, is myself. I've had a lifetime to avoid myself. We all have.

Instagram: Thelma_and_Disease
Twitter: Racheddar

Chapter 29

Where There's a Will

By Billie Jo Gillispie

I'd been doing comedy just under a year, when I began my time away. I wasn't any good, yet, or a regular, on the scene. I already knew it was a path I wanted to continue. I had to put comedy on the back burner, the day my toxic relationship got violent. I had nowhere to go, but was leaving, any way possible. I saw no possible way to stay with any friends, so I didn't ask. The Marine Corps had taught me how to acknowledge my fear, and continue, in spite of it. Adams county doesn't have any services for the homeless, so I had the choice of going urban, in Denver, or in the woods, outside of Boulder, where the crime rate is lowest in the nation.

June 3, I arrived in Boulder, having walked away from my life, without a word to anyone. It was a Friday afternoon, so I had to wait until Monday, to find out what I could do about my situation. My situation being that my wallet had been stolen. I had no identification, to be able to get a job, or medical attention, etc. How do you prove who you are, to get the process started, to reclaim my identity? When I had asked that question, at the Thornton DMV, they offered to have me arrested.

I was in Boulder 2 weeks, before I found out my son had filed a missing persons report. I reached out to my kids, at that time, explaining what happened and why I wouldn't tell anyone where I had gone. Another month, and I reached out to a friend, who had, of course heard from my wife about how she wanted her family back together. My friend has helped people leave violent relationships before. There was no worry of her telling my wife where I was. She immediately let me know she wanted to come see that I was ok.

One of the hardest things about this, wasn't the sleeping outside, or the having to choose between an appointment, and the opportunity for a meal, it was running in to people who you have known, over the years. I lived clean, even behind an electric box.

The 50 liter backpack was a gave away that I was living outside. Once that was noticed, I might as well have had leprosy. It sucks to find out people you once respected, will treat you so snobbishly.

The process of getting my identity back, was slow. I had my birth certificate. With direction from a case manager at the Boulder Bridge House, I was able to get the process started. I would go to a government agency, to request a piece of paper, to take to another government agency, to request another piece of paper. The whole time, a question I had had go unanswered at the DMV burned in my mind. When you get a license, you are finger printed, for the one finger. Why can't I use that to prove who I am, for a new ID? I began the Monday after arriving, and was waiting for things to come in the mail, until September. It took 3 months once I found the path. I had been trying on my own, for 8 months. If I had been able to work, I would have felt comfortable, asking a friend, to stay on their couch.

I was camping with a group, enjoying safety in numbers. One night, raccoons came for a visit. Most of the people on my side of the porch where we slept didn't bring food to camp. Apparently, the other side of the porch had a different view about food. The raccoons had so much fun flipping everything over under the porch and going through people's stuff, it sounded like they were throwing furniture. I woke, and sat up, to see where the noise was coming from. I saw fellow camper, who we call Canada, looking around too. I realize, at that moment, that if they get startled, and come our way, I am in front of the exit. I reached down, under the porch, and grabbed a stick. I didn't sleep, the rest of the night, waiting for the need to defend myself.

By the middle of July, I had all the magic pieces of paper, and was able to get through the DMV's hoops. My ID and social security card were on the way. I found a program to help homeless people get back to work. I jumped on that, since I wasn't sure I could get a job, with a day shelter for an address, and with no phone. I got started, just before our camp got found, and I lost my things, to the police. I now had no clothes and no sleeping bag. I still got up, and went to work, through the challenge of getting things replaced. There are programs that help homeless people get gear and clothes. Since it happened while I was working, it didn't help me. I spent most of July and August being promised help replacing, at least, my sleeping bag. That would have been nice, but that person never remembered to do so. My first check came on my birthday. My wallet was stolen, that same night. I worked hard to get that ID, I was furious to have to repeat any of those steps. I was a little pissed, when the Boulder DMV did allow me to use my fingerprint, and little else, to replace it. I wasn't mad at Boulder, but the charming lady working the desk, in Thornton.

In August, I was able, to move from the landscape crew, of the Ready To Work program, to the brand new, commercial kitchen, the Bridge House was just beginning to use. I had never worked in a brand spanking new kitchen, with 100% new, everything. It was beautiful. Everything was shiny and worked. It was every cooks dream.

Life was getting better, until it rained for days. On the 4th night of rain, I had run out of dry places to sleep. I slept on a hill, with my tarp acting as a funnel, one night. I woke up, in a puddle, one night. I sought refuge from the rain, in the apartment of someone who had recently gotten off the streets. She had several women staying with her that night. I was the only one not drunk or wanting to fight. When the city emergency warning system started to sound, I was glad to be indoors. Unfortunately, No one could hear the announcement with it, over the screaming of one of the women.

That next morning, I got in touch with another member of the Ready to Work team and was told we weren't working that day. That's when I learned that what I missed, was the 14 foot wall of water, that came down the canyon. We were experiencing a flood. Staying in the apartment with no food or coffee, but plenty of alcohol was the first really bad day, of homelessness. The next day, I let the nutrition director know I would be at work.

I managed to stay 3 nights in the apartment, before the drama got to me. I set out to find a dry place to sleep. I ended up having to get even more creative than the camping ban already dictated. I found a temporary spot that was flat, and dark, and stayed for as long as it existed. I was glad to find that tiny place, since the homeless shelter chose not to open.

Donations came our way, fast and furious, after the flood. Entire pallets of gear, for homeless came from as far away as Pennsylvania. My sleeping bag was finally replaced. There were days, that my gear got upgraded several times. I handed people good gear, that I had been thankful for, that morning, because I had just scored better.

Before the flood, it felt like late summer. Afterward, fall had arrived, and I wondered if I was ready for outdoor winter in Boulder. The shelter only allows 90 nights, and winter is longer than that. The next payday, I spent most of my check, to get prepared. People freeze to death, in the summer here. I was not going into winter, without knowing I could survive.

The first snow came in October. By then, I had a two person tent, and a sleeping bag that was great for summer. I had a fuzzy blanket, which gave me more warmth than the sack. I had a paycheck, so I had hope, as I saved to get off the streets. I wasn't ready to start spending my 90 nights, when the shelter opened for the year. I was able to go there to shower, and have breakfast, in the morning. At that time I was happy using those services.

The shelter felt familiar, like a squad bay, so I was able to rest when I signed up for their program in October. I was able to get a great sleeping bag, and warm gear, when November rolled around. The government has a program to help get necessary equipment to unhoused veterans. I was able to take part, since my proof of service had arrived, people quit rolling their eyes, about me being a Marine.

January 21st, I didn't backdown to someone threatening me, and was booted for 30 days. As I stood in front of the shelter, watching the snow fall, I tried to figure out what to do. My buddy Matt was headed in the shelter, and asked, "What's Up?" "Now what? Where are you going to sleep?" He had me wait, while he went to his locker, to get what he needed. When he got back he had a plan, and I liked it. "You're just going to have to stay with me and John, tonight. We have a tent, you'll be safe and dry. I never expected 3 adults could fit in a 2 person tent, but we managed for 3 nights. Then found an SUV I could sleep in, for the month. It was a colder than usual February with 3 week record breaking cold snap. Coldest night was -21 degrees. That morning I went to unzip, only to find I had been breathing on my zipper and needed to break the ice . My boots were frozen to the inside of sack. When I arrived at work, that morning, my boss was visibly relieved.

When I went to stay at the shelter, again, they told me I only had a few nights left, before hitting my 90 night limit. I would soon be back to hunting for places to hide, for rest. My time with the Ready to Work program came to an end in March. Now, I was jobless, homeless, and wondering what I had accomplished. I ended up working with a temp service that mostly does construction clean up, and other shitty jobs. My housing had come through, now I had to find a place to live, and a job that I could get back and forth, by bus. I had just about decided I wouldn't find a place, when my VA case manager told me about a place for rent, in Lafayette. I got on the bus with the attitude that I hoped I liked it, because I was taking it. I moved in (my sleeping bag) May 1, 2014.

Coming back to comedy was very much starting over, having lost my joke book. I see where this experience has changed my approach. I have way more hustle than I ever would have imagined. It also makes sleeping in the car easy while on the road.

Instagram: BillieJoGillispieComedy

Chapter 30

Mark Masters

By Mark Masters

Mark Masters is my stage name.

It isn't real. My actual name is ... well, that's none of your business.

I think most audiences realize Mark Masters is a stage name. Unless they think my parents were hoping for an adult entertainment star. Or a magician.

Some say the name is hacky. I like to think of it as memorable. An alliteration. Like that last sentence.

On stage, my stage name and I have been through a lot together. Off stage, we have our own identity and history. Which is surprising for a name I only asked to be memorable.

We'll get back to that, but let's start in the beginning. 2018 was my first year of stand up. It was a lot of fun, but awful too.

You meet a lot of great people. But you fail. Over and over. In public. For me and my stage name, that was mostly in noisy dive bars around Denver.

I spent a lot of time waiting in these places. Hours sometimes, for just a few minutes of mic time. And the hardest waits were the late ones.

One good thing about waiting when your material is weak, is there is almost no one left to hear you. A host. A disinterested bartender. If you are lucky, one or two other sad souls. One bad thing about waiting when you crave stage time and experience, is there is almost no one left to hear you.

I did a lot of waiting in one venue in particular. Lion's Lair on Colfax Avenue. The longest running comedy open mic in Denver. It is one of the hardest too, because the vibe can be ... unfriendly. I remember the first time I ever went. A host suggested another comedian should quit. Over the microphone. For all to hear.

The disinterest from other comedians can be acute. Most nights the comedians get as far from the stage as possible. Probably if they could hide under the pinball machine (The Shadow, 1994) they would.

For me the most difficult aspect is the late start, 11PM. Once I had a 6AM flight the next day. I badly wanted to go on stage early. But I didn't. The hosts at this mic pick names off the list however they like. I went up after all the names that were better known than mine. Few of which stuck around to see me struggle.

One time at Lion's Lair though, magic struck. I was called up early.

It was admittedly a feat of luck, no skill required. But when I got that chance, you better believe I took everything I had learned in more than fifty open mic experiences, to make the most of it.

Those experiences were at Denver bars like the White Whale, Irish Rover, Lincoln Station, 3 Kings, Syntax Physic Opera, and Black Buzzard. Great places if you compare them to the bars I arrived at to find the mic delayed, cancelled, or more often than I care to admit, the venue permanently closed.

I can't over express my gratitude for the hosts of these mics who wait more than anyone else. They have to listen to every comic no matter how bad. They are the enablers of comedic exploration, and sometimes, but rarely, some of it is good.

My formative open mic experiences impacted what I did at Lion's Lair that night. But why was I called up so early? My first clue was revealed on the road.

I traveled to Atlanta to volunteer at, and attend, the Red Clay Comedy Festival. Some Denver comics were performing. Nathan Lund, Allison Rose, Geoff Tice and Jeff Koehn. I would end up making a gift bag for Janeane Garofalo among other duties. But first I had to find someone to tell me what to do.

My volunteer coordinator was running late on day one, and tried to contact me on Facebook. A communication hub for almost every comedian.

But not me. Even today I've never been on it. Real name. Stage name. Any name. Never.

But in a classic Who's On First situation, she found another Denver based comedian named Mark Masters. He promptly Facebook messaged her back and confusion ensued. Once it cleared, he informed her that he had heard of this other Mark Masters.

And he made sure to tell her that he was in Denver at home for a reason. The newer Mark Masters, so he had heard, was funnier. I couldn't believe it. Not only was there another Denver comic named Mark Masters, there must be a third one as well!

The festival was incredible, and I had a great time. I learned a ton from other comics. Once back in Denver I continued my first year slog. Writing. Performing. Failing. Getting back up again. Wash. Rinse. Repeat.

I thought I had heard the end of other Denver comics named Mark Masters. But I was wrong. My stage name had one more trick for me.

It was a chilly fall night just after Halloween, and I was at Lion's Lair. My late arrival didn't discourage me from scrawling Mark Masters at the end of the list. As I found a stool at the bar, I noticed a buzz amongst the comics. And not because it was the time T.J. Miller dropped in.

This time touring comic and local legend Sam Tallent was on hand, to co-host with Byron Graham. Early on Byron disappeared into the back room. Sam was left solo. He looked at the list to call up another comic and said:

"It's been awhile since I've seen this guy, let's welcome Mark Masters to the stage"

He was not talking about me. We had never met. But was I

going to let that confusion stop me? No way! I rushed to the stage.

The place was packed, even up front, nobody had left yet. I stared out at the crowd, microphone in hand. Sam looked at me, quizzically. I stared into the distance, a bit overwhelmed.

A moment of quiet ensued.

I finally broke the silence. Progressed through my jokes. Told my stories. Sharpened by hours of stage time. Earned a few minutes at a time, over many months, in numerous venues. Slung some new stuff too.

I wouldn't say I crushed the room. But, I got some compliments after, and earned a couple good laughs from the back wall comics. Many of whom had never stuck around to see me before.

Even better, I felt great the next day. Refreshed by a decent night's sleep.

2018 was the year I told my very first joke on any stage. I performed at Comedy Works downtown ahead of Josh Blue. Did stage time in six states. I even did a showcase set in New York City.

But the highlight may have been that night at Lion's Lair. Getting on stage early and meeting Sam Tallent.

All because of a name.

Website: www.markmasters.co
Book: www.notgoodyet.com (Now on Audible!)

Chapter 31

Editor Feedback on COVID-19 Yearbook Spread

By Hannah Jones

Hey Meg,

First off, thanks for all of your hard work on this year's yearbook committee! I wasn't exaggerating when I said this spread could end up in museums someday, and I hope you'll understand that that's why my critical revisions are so extensive. Here are my thoughts on your COVID-19 themed pages:

1. The header line "virtual learning for our virtual futures." While I love the play on words here, what if it said "virtual learning for our real futures"? I know we disagree on this, but I think your future is very bright and we won't experience a climate apocalypse before you reach adulthood. I think the yearbook should reflect that optimism!

2. Your choice to include a blurb about Amanda Pate fighting with her drunk parents during quarantine felt like it crossed the line from effective human interest into invasion of privacy. In general, I would prefer to not include screenshots of Tiktoks at all, particularly when the subjects are crying!

3. While I felt you annotated the larger group picture in a creative way, I don't think it's entirely necessary to include evidence of Crestview students refusing to social distance properly, and I definitely don't love the decision to caption it "shame them!"

4. I felt the bulk of the editorial copy on the right side was pretty concerning in both tone and content, and as a mandatory reporter I did refer it to your guidance counselor.

5. I didn't find the "no school shootings for two months!" bit funny at all.

6. LOVED the collage of art students wearing their hand-painted N95s. We should change the copy from "enough masks for upper class prep schoolers but not for our nation's nurses and doctors???????" to something like "creativity in the darkest of

times!"

7. The screenshots of zoom classes were fun, but we obviously can't include the one that was Zoom-bombed with Hentai enthusiasts.

8. The left lower corner includes the blurb "online bullying still causes offline pain!" as well as multiple screenshots of behavior that ccurred outside of Crestview leadership's knowledge or jurisdiction. Definitely wouldn't be fair to have that reflect poorly on our staff. Great tag though!

9. Animal Crossing is not a nationally recognized e-sport and Crestview does not have an official Animal Crossing program. For this next draft, let's focus on silver linings and optimism and representing Crestview pride! Go bulldogs!

Thanks,
Ms. Cherry

Instagram, Twitter and Venmo: HannahJonesCool

Chapter 32

(This is an excerpt from Cal Sheridan's future project, "Cal Sheridan: In My Element")

Cal Observes Things

By Cal Sheridan

"Cultural appropriation; it's a horrible thing. I don't think I'll ever know the true pain it causes. However, I believe I do have somewhat of an idea... Because evidently... you able-bodied folks are now fuckin' around on electric scooters?! That's OUR thing!! You can walk AND drive, why do you need a scooter?!

And furthermore, you're using an electric scooter STANDING UP. That's like the ULTIMATE 'fuck you' to disabled people! It's an electric scooter that we can't even use!! You know, we didn't LAND on the sidewalk. The sidewalk landed on us!!"

"Let's go to something a bit lighter: Police reform! I think we should replace ALL the cops in the US... with clowns. Think about it! We could saveso much tax money on cop cars, because we could fit a whole squadron in ONE car!! Plus how else are we gonna combat the rising threat of Juggalos? The only way to stop anINSane Clown Posse, is with a Sane Clown Posse!!"

My favorite famous comedians are Iliza Shlesinger, Jim Gaffigan, Sarah Silverman (circa 2017), Brian Regan, and yes... Jerry Seinfeld. These people are all VERY different, but they have a few things in common:

1) They are all distinct. You wouldn't confuse a Brian Regan joke with anyone else's. That's his style. Same with Iliza — each of these comedians I've listed have completely different stage presence and joke telling styles from anyone else.

2) In my words, they are all "highly observational". I find comedy to be funniest when it takes a look at this strange, strange world we clothe-wearing animals have built ourselves. And it doesn't necessarily in a deep or profound way. Jim Gaffigan isn't trying to change the

world with his comedy like Sarah Silverman does in her latest work, but they both enjoy pointing out its flaws and hypocrisies.

And that's the reason why this, first and foremost, is my goal. Not two peoples' perspectives are exactly the same, and I desire to give mine, because y'all... Being on earth? Being surrounded by other living things,and interacting with some of them? THAT'S a very weird situation! That'sIMPOSSIBLY weird! That's basically the theme of every sitcom for kidsAND adults!! "Living things interact, SHENANIGANS!!". Life on Earth as ahuman is like watching a sit com but everything is happening to you. It's EXTREMELY comedic!!

And from MY point of view, it's even weirder, because I have a very unique point from which to see things. Quite literally, as I watch the world from the perspective of sitting down. In fact, that may be the reason I have such acute observational skills. I didn't talk in full sentences until I was 5 years old (y'know, cerebral palsy and all that), so I basically had to watch everything happen! It was like watching a 4D movie. You feel and see everything, but you can't interact with it. You can't say I wasn't a patient kid!!

Because of my unique point of view, I notice things, but perhaps I think about them a bit differently than you. For example, all comedians do jokes about air travel, because to put it mildly, air travel is far from the most relaxing process one can experience. However, in my repertoire, there's a joke about how things can get even more complicated with a mobility device. "You would think that they'd take extra care of something so valuable to your everyday life," I say, and then take a deep breath, maybe laugh lightly... "YOU. WOULD. THINK." I scream with the fury of the gods. "And yet, you'd be WRONG!!! They LOSE it, they leave it on the FUCKING JET BRIDGE. They BREAK IT. TWICE. IN ONE TRIP!!!" But of course, that means very little to the audience of mostly able bodies.

They've never dealt with any of this! I'm normally the only one in the room with a scooter, and chances are, I'm the only person with a scooter they've ever heard do stand-up! So I must provide context. I must equivocate my experience to something that might happen to them. So, I go, "Imagine you're getting off the plane, ready to leave this whole airplane experience behind you, and then a gate agent comes up to you and BREAKS YOUR FUCKING LEGS!! Wouldn't you be pretty pissed?"

For many people, I'm probably the only person with a disability they've heard talk about their disability. I'm the ambassador to my audience from the dyskinetic, dystonic cerebral palsy world. I'm not saying people HAVEN'T done what I'm doing. In fact, there's a surprising amount of comedians with cerebral palsy. Josh Blue, Christie Buchele, "Lost Voice Guy" from England... It's practically become a stereotype, just look at Jimmy from South Park! But we're still a literal minority. Cerebral palsy isn't talked about in the mainstream, it's not shown. We JUST got a television show, Speechless, and it JUST got cancelled. And as such, people honestly may just not be familiar with CP, or my perspective and way of life. I don't claim to speak for all people with cerebral palsy, but I can speak for me. (Except for on stage, 'cuz I have people read for me)

That said, though, if we were in the mainstream, I'm pretty sure the disabled community as a whole would breathe a sigh of relief. Our stories would get told, so we wouldn't need to tell able bodied people when they ask stupid questions. We'd normalize disability, which is what we all want. We don't want to be asked "Are you okay?" when simply walking down the street! The answer to that question, by the way, is always, "Well, I was until YOU showed up!!"

And that's kinda why I like doing this — saying things, entertaining people and showing them my perspective. I want to bring disability into the limelight. I want to help future generations of disabled people by educating and normalizing disability. I want to be an entertainer, not just for me (although, y'know, mostly for me), but also for the future. I'd love to be the hero for one little kid in a wheelchair who watches a soap opera on accident, and sees me shoot my fraternal twin brother out the window. And the little kid would be like, "Mommy! Mommy! That guy has a scooter too!!".

And the mom would turn to her child and say... "What were you doing watching a violent daytime drama? This is wildly inappropriate."

YouTube: Cal Sheridan

Chapter 33

Join the Undead Legion for better Orgasms.

By Nyland Vigil

Author's Note: I read Stewart Lee's collection of prose titled Content Provider, and instantly fell in love with satire. Specifically posing as editorial articles. So I began writing and submitting my own satire with no publishing success to speak of. I had been told my writing was too psychotic and nonsensical and, most egregious of all, not click-bait.

I took those notes into consideration and begrudgingly wrote what was my first published satire. To be honest it was an infantile tantrum, a cynical retaliation born out of my bruised ego, but they accepted it anyway. I wonder if this one was accepted because I'm funnier when I'm angry or because publishers have a dim view of the public and my shittier writing would be well received.

Nonetheless, my favorite aspect of comedy writing remains defending absurdity with the pretense of art. Mice with big dicks in 18th century hats are to be admired, not disregarded. Which hat did you just think of?

There seems to be no consensus on Denver's dating landscape. Wallet Hub recently named Denver one of the best cities to find love, while the Great Love Debate Podcast calls it the worst. However an influx of young people has undoubtedly caused two things to rise; Rent and Rough Sex. Some people may be new to the concepts of choking, flogging, throttling, bottling or the move that has come to be known in some circles as "The Pain Turducken". But for many locals, a lot of these new practices are already old hat. So what's left once you've done the electric slide with real electricity? I may have a suggestion.

1874 was a big year for the development of Denver. It was the year that the towns people of Denver banded together to drive out the Western Dust Vampires from the underground tunnels in River North. It also happened to be the same year that the

Denver Art Museum landed here from space, and soon after plans were laid for the construction of the Capitol building. For the past 140 years Denver has kept an arms length policy with all things supernatural. Local government officials have been known to shut down art exhibitions in RINO. I suspect for the purpose of keeping the old Dust Vampire Catacombs closed. But what if the answer to Denver's vanillification happens to be right under our very feet?

It's well known that no one climaxes like a night leech. So much so that the Vampir are often rumored to have sexual brainwashing powers. However the Dark Magic Index 5th edition only lists their abilities as anti-aging, Therianthropy and the ability to turn wine into Tequila. We can only assume the rumor is based on nothing more in raw physical attraction.

Executive order 121 from the office of mayor Hancock 3.0 Rule C states trade and fraternization with Hemosexual Nocturnal Undead is prohibited. However I can find no evidence of this executive order ever being enforced directly. Blood tasting parties are easily attended through apps like Meet-up and Denver's Kink community is home to many Vampire.

I purpose we embrace our nocturnal neighbors to keep our growing mile high metropolis interesting and sexual gratified. Making the Vampire a staple of Denver's eccentric culture could have added benefits of increased commerce and their supernatural powers may come in handy if the vegetable-monsters growing in boulder ever decided to attack the city. For more information on that refer to the article "Boulder Ents are actually Dryad vegetable-monsters."

Phone: 720-795-4692

Chapter 34

Cranksgiving

By Piper Shephard

It was my first month living in Seattle and Thanksgiving was just around the corner. I had never spent Thanksgiving away from my family before, and I was excited for this new chapter in my life and my first holiday outside of family tradition. I had moved into part of the storage shed of a house in the U-District. It was dingy and narrow with no air conditioning unit, but small enough that a space heater could easily heat up the whole room. I had my own key and was able to lock the door upon leaving and entering. There was a wooden board that came out of the wall, shaped for a bed to go on. The girl who ran the house found an old futon mattress in the alley and brought it in for me to use as a bed. The springs were all discombobulated and it was only comfortable to sleep on from a certain angle that I could never maintain because it was constantly sliding around. I found a mirror and a small dresser to put in there, and my room was officially set up.

I had gotten a job at a botanical place on the south side of town, in the holiday department, assembling Christmas decorations. I had to wake up at 4:30 in the morning to catch the bus to make it to work by 6 am every day, which turned my sleeping schedule into a living nightmare, but on the bright side, it was less time I had to spend in the shed.

The actual house was referred to as the Hobbit House. It was very old and has a woodland faerie-esque charm about it. It was set for demolition in early 2020, and I had been invited to live there for its last days. The house was occupied by seven other tenants, and the rent was incredibly cheap.

Everyone kept to themselves for the most part, though I was friends with two of the housemates, Mercy and Nick. They loved spending time with me and keeping me up late even though I had to wake up at 4 every morning. I was tired and hungover all the time, rarely making it to work when I was supposed to, but the situation was manageable enough. That is until when one classic holiday turned everything on its head and spiraled completely out of control.

When Thanksgiving rolled around, there was no shortage of plans and options on how to spend it. Personally, I had some other friends in the city who had already invited me to Thanksgiving dinner at their house, one that was a lot newer and nicer than mine. The Hobbit House had its own plan concocted. They were planning a Danksgiving where 100% of the food would be pot-infused. I did not make plans to witness it.

I wake up in my storage shed early in the morning on Thanksgiving day, waiting for the time to pass until I can Uber over to my dinner plans. I FaceTimed my family back in Denver for a while, then got up and went into the house. No one was up or around except for Nick, who was spry and chipper and ready for the day. He was so excited about Danksgiving, and naturally assumed I would be attending.

Now this was going to be tricky. While I had no intention on actually attending Danksgiving, I didn't want to hurt anyone's feelings. So I walked over to the grocery store, bought two pies, and two six packs. I returned and told Nick that I purchased pie and booze for each house, and that I planned on hopping around to multiple Thanksgiving dinners. Eventually I was able to make my break and fled to the other dinner, where I proceeded to get so fucked up I was there well into Friday evening. But nevertheless, I had work at 6 am the next morning, and had to go home to get some sleep.

When I arrived back at the shed, I noticed on the other side, three people smoking meth. I, being totally wasted and having to get up early, decided to ignore it and go straight to bed, door locked.

The next morning I was woken up by the sounds of Mercy and the three kids arguing. Mercy asked them to please leave,

"I invited you over for a nice meal and a warm place to sleep! I did not say you guys could power smoke meth in the shed all night!"

One of the guys, Thomas, had been occupying that space a few days prior to all of this, and was working on his bike. He seemed nice enough a few days ago when I met him, but had a clear change of attitude at this point. Apparently while I was gone they invited over his ex-girlfriend, Riley, and their friend Lorenzo, an ex-con who had just gotten out of prison. The three of them were all homeless meth heads. I am listening to the drama go down from behind my locked door.

"We're not leaving. You can't make us leave! I'll call the cops on you!"

"You? Call the cops on me? This is MY HOUSE! I'll call the cops on you!"

One of the tweakers goes, "Everybody back up! I have bear mace. I'll mace you right in the face!"

"You have to leave. This is not your space. I didn't say you could stay in the shed. I invited you here!"

"Back the FUCK up!"

At this point, Thomas has taken a blunt object and starts breaking down the door. Riley pulls out a plastic makeup scalpel, throws it on the ground, and is beating the shit out of Mercy. Lorenzo flees the scene. Everything goes quiet for a few minutes. Thinking that the coast was clear, I walked in the house and took a seat in the living room. Upon sitting down a police officer made eyes with me through the window outside. He pointed at me and mouthed the words, "Do you live here?" Behind him was a whole line of police officers, about ten or twelve total. They knocked on the front door,

"Is Trisha in there? Do you grant us permission to come into the house to speak to Trisha? Do you give us your permission to come inside the house?"

"Well yeah, I suppose so, I mean do I really have a choice?" I said. Then I went downstairs and told Mercy that the cops would like to speak with her.

"Oh I would LOVE to speak to them!" she said.

Riley and Thomas were standing in the front yard talking to the cops. Riley had black eye makeup running down her face from crying.

"This woman called us to report that the girl Trisha threatened her with a scalpel."

Okay, so the tweakers called the cops on Mercy, whose real name is Trisha, because she asked them to leave. I see.

"No," I told the police, "I was in my room listening to everything that was happening outside, and that did not happen. From what I heard, that guy was threatening to spray everyone in the face with bear mace. After that I heard them begin to chop the door down, then everyone fled the scene."

Mercy chimes in, "Officer, the scalpel she is referring to is a plastic makeup scalpel. I am a street performer and I use them to apply my makeup. If I were going to threaten someone, it would be with my three inch knife, not a flimsy piece of plastic.

I invited the guy over two nights ago for Thanksgiving dinner, because he's homeless, and I wanted to give him a warm and safe place to sleep for the night. I did not invite Riley, I would not have been okay with it had I known she was coming over. Then Lorenzo showed up and the three of them all decided to start smoking meth in the shed.

They all have tons of drugs. I can show you where they are. They're right over there."

The police chimed in, "Ma'am, we were not called on a drug offense. We were called on a domestic violence offense. We're not worried about the drugs."

"Well again officer, why would I threaten someone with a flimsy piece of plastic instead of my actual weapon? If I was gonna threaten someone, I would threaten someone with something effective. That girl Riley is lying and they refuse to leave my house."

"Ma'am, this woman is saying you have invited them over to your house before."

"Once, yeah, in the past. I don't see what that has to do with anything."

"Well technically if you invite someone into your home they have a right to stay.."

"That can't be right. There's no way that's the law."

"Anyway there's not really much we can do other than ask them to leave. If they come back you'll just have to call us again."

So eventually, the cops leave. The tweakers leave. I talk to Mercy about what just went down. We smoke many cigarettes. I already texted my boss and told her I wasn't coming in due to police investigating a "home invasion" at our house. I go back to sleep in much distress.

I woke up later that evening to discover the tweakers had come back, and the cops were called again, and they were asked to leave again. Mercy hands me a five dollar bill and asks me if I will go down to the smoke shop and buy her some rolling tobacco. She's afraid if she goes, she'll get jumped by the tweakers. But they don't have any ill will towards me, so I'll be fine. She begs me until I finally agree to make the tobacco run. I walk with pure fear running through my bones. I feel a million miles away from Denver now.

Twitter and Instagram: Exorcistasy
YouTube & Facebook: Piper Shepherd
Website:
https://pipershepherdfreaks.wixsite.com/pipershepherd

Chapter 35

Voices You Don't Normally Hear From

By Jose Macall

Fanfiction tends to be about the heros and main characters of the story, which as we all know tends to follow a narrow group of archetypes (Grizzled cop, handsome person in leadership position, down and out grizzled cop in a leadership position, etc.). I have taken it upon myself to write from the viewpoints of people you don't normally hear from in the story. I present to you interviews with the other people who were also there, or Bystander Fiction:

Agnes Perlmutter, who almost bought a ticket to the Titanic:
"Oh my goodness. That was quite a tragedy. I was a-peelin' onions and talkin' to the neighbor Missus Grambleman. We were talkin' about the War and the Kaiser and whether or not he got his fortune because of the bread rolls. I brought up I was a-thinkin' about going on that there big ol' boat cause it seemed so luxurious and I could do with a vacation. Well Missus Grambleman told me that she thought it was better I stay on the land like a good god-fearin' Christian and that I wasn't Noah. I said Missus Grambleman you are too much! Boy, I can't wait to eat these onions in some onion soup. Let me tell you, that soup was so delicious. The secret to a good onion soup is hot water. You want the heat to make the broth warm so it cooks the ingredients. Now what were we talkin' about again sweetie?"

Wanda Washington, passenger on the Speed bus:
"Oh boy, I'm glad that lil' white boy came and saved everybody. I was really surprised the police department showed up so fast, that wasn't the first time I saw a bus driver get shot. Last time it took'em twenty-five minutes to get there. I for sure thought we were all gonna die. I can't be having all these crazy adventures on the Metro. One time I saw a fight between a man dressed like a clown and the dude that sells burritos. They were rolling around on the ground, punching and screaming. There was a lot of biting too, but that's how you eat a burrito. (Wanda took several minutes to stop laughing at her own joke.) Anyway, that

bus thing was wild. Can you believe that the Metro people didn't even give me a refund for how bad that ride was?"

The last wIldebeest in the Lion King who is way behind the rest of the pack inside the gorge where Mufasa died:
"Listen, stampeding isn't the easiest thing in the world. First of all, I was going to the bathroom behind a bush, I heard the herd start to stampede but I wanted to finish up. I enjoy privacy. I know you think we just go all over, like we're uncivilized but that's an unfair depiction that the documentary-industrial complex uses to unfairly portray us. Anyway, everyone knows that you have to follow the herd, so of course, even if I was late, I still stampeded. I ran, but I had no idea that the king was dead. I don't even get why the other Wildebeests ran him over, they were at his baby shower a few weeks before that! They totally would have recognized him. Like, even if the first guy in the stampede missed it, by like the sixth, seventh, hundredth guy, one of them has to be like Hey that big-ass cat we're all trampling looks strangely like the dude in charge of everything we all pay protection money to. It's a little strange is all I'm saying... Look I may have said too much already... Boy, those invitations to Simba's kids' Pride Rock reveal were pretty awkward."

Ralph Patterson, who got the hell out of Nakatomi Plaza as soon as the shooting started:
"I knew something was up when the gunshots started. People were at that party upstairs, I coulda gone up there to investigate, but they just paid me to clean the bathrooms, ya know? What do they want me to do? I can only mop the floor with the guy if he's got his own bucket, you know what I mean? I ran the hell out of there. Should I have pulled the fire alarm? I mean it technically wasn't a fire. Is gunfire a fire? I don't wanna get fined for cryin' wolf or whatever, ya know what I mean? I clean up messes but not like this, knowaddamean? I figure security could take care of it. Is there a bad guy alarm, you think? I bet the guards don't even gotta call 911. They probably gotta special line straight to the chief, ya know? Anyway, since that building blew up I lost my janitor gig. I got my own shop vac business now. I hear shootin', I'm outta there. Do you have any semblance of knowledge to what my meaning is, though?"

Frank Barrens, the guy everyone forgot was still plugged into the

Matrix:
"Today was a great day. It's my one day off a week! Went to the store, got half priced dairy creamer. Had some coffee, relaxed in front of the TV, went out for a jog, and ate a sandwich. Boy, I have a long one coming up tomorrow, I should get to bed early. Everything's hunky dory."

Phil, from New York, in the background of most movies:
"GET OUTTA THE FREAKIN WAY I'M TRYNNA GET TA DA FREAKIN' SUBWAY AND EAT A FREAKIN' BAGEL!"

One of the sandpeople from Star Wars:
(This interview was cut short due to the violent nature of the sand person. If anyone has information on the whereabouts of our interviewer, please notify the national center for missing persons.)

Jilly Watermacher, who lived near where those people who played Jumanji here at:
"I saw a monkey driving a car! And a Rhinoceros! And a Gorilla. And a Giraffe! I saw all the plants get really big, my daddy had to cut them. He likes to cut the lawn. His name is Harold. He cries when mommy yells at him. One day I want to play Jaminji."

Jubley Daisytaster, who lived on the other side of Middle-Earth:
 "Oh really, they had a war over there? Sounds grisly, that business."

Owen Racker, who lived on Oak Street:
"Boy, those fuckers on Elm Street are crazy as hell, eh? I moved to Springwood because I thought this was a nice little cozy town to settle down, finally retire from hunting maple bandits. Suddenly all the kids are gettin' sleep murdered. I says This is madness. Not even Newfoundlanders act like this. I mean, even when I was up in Canada hunting maple bandits, I never ran into something so crazy as all the teenagers start dying overnight. Sometimes they get crushed by a maple tree, mauled by a bear, or shot by maple bandits, but never just sleep dyin'. That's craziness. Worst thing that happened here on Oak Street is the neighbor two houses down got slapped by his wife for

foolin' around on the side. You think it's too soon to make a move on her?"

Steve Overton, who was laid off from Jurassic Park:
"Oh the benefits sounded great. It was really my dream job and apparently someone dropped the ball on quality control. That's what I heard. The whole thing went under. I didn't even get my first paycheck. I thought Oh God, I have to go back to the magic kingdom, I can't do this... Fortunately I now manage at Primordial Park which is a way easier job and pays far better. It's a lot of sludges and slimes, and mosses. Nothing that's going to break out of a fence and bite through a visitor. The worst that happens here is someone breaks into the enclosure and slips on the exhibit. People just love to come see these goo puddles for some reason."

Thank you for taking this time to consider the viewpoints of others.

Podcast: mixlr.com/threeam
Instagram: Macall4info

Chapter 36

Cute-Ass Cat

By Lauren Dufault

Damn
I wish I was a cute ass cat.
maybe in a cute ass hat
One that got a million likes
and million toys.
Id be really good at that.

I would chew up all the tissue paper
and hiss at the next door neighbor
Id sleep on your face
in the middle of the night
but you wouldn't get mad because Im so fucking cute, right?

I would throw up on your favorite rug
and even shit in bath tub
And you know what you'd think?
"Look at this cute ass cat,
 I could never hate her like that"

And when I would get sick and tired
of you and your human bullshit.
Id hide in your closet
maybe take another shit.
And when the next day comes
and you want to wear that thing I sat in
You'd look at me
and I'd purr back
and you'd do nothing about it
because Im a cute ass mother fucking cat.

Meow.

Instagram: LaurenDufault

Chapter 37

MY PONY RAN BUT STUMBLED

BY BEN BRYANT

EXT. AMERICAN WEST

A GUNSLINGER(20s, female, cowfolk attire) rides a HORSE across the picturesque western landscape, surveying the land.

                GUNSLINGER
    (to horse) Juss' a few more days 'fore
               California.

As the Gunslinger crests a hill to see a DISTANT PLAINS HOUSE, something RUSTLES in the nearby bushes. The Gunslinger draws her gun.

A beat. Music sting.

Nothing is there.

She goes to holster her gun, and spins it around in a bunch of fancy, ridiculous, ways (over the head, between the legs, bounces it off the ground like a basketball etc).

She drops the gun. Her horse steps on it, and causes a shot to FIRE, and the horse to buck.

                GUNSLINGER
        Whoa! Ya fuckin' horse!

Panicking, the horse steps on the gun many more times. One of the shots whizzes by the Gunslinger's head, tearing a hole in her hat.

                GUNSLINGER
      So it's a fight yer wantin'?

The Gunslinger produces a small pistol from her boot and opens fire on the horse she's riding. The bucking stops. She shoots again. Again. Three times. She keeps firing. More shots ring out. It's a lot. Many more than a pistol should be able to carry.

CUT TO:

EXT. PLAINS HOUSE

MORT (60s, male, gruff) sits on the porch, rocking in his chair.
The Gunslinger approaches, dragging the horse in long, rhythmic pulls.

> GUNSLINGER
> 'Scuse me!

She continues to drag the horse with considerable effort. REVEAL a long trail of BLOOD and HORSE BONES trailing from her descent. She finally drags the horse to the foot of the porch.

> GUNSLINGER
> Sir, kin ya help me? Mah horse was injured during our ride.

The horse coughs up MANY BULLETS.

> GUNSLINGER
> (aside) Quiet you!

Mort takes a long draw from his pipe. No response.

> GUNSLINGER
> Hello?

Mort exhales. Then takes a bigger, longer draw

of his pipe.

The horse looks up at Mort in what seems to be desperation.

                        MORT
Nothing here to fix up ponies, sorry. There's a general store about... (he exhales, then checks his watch) 30 miles down the way.

                   GUNSLINGER
       (sighs) Ok. Thank ye kindly.

She tips her hat, and begins dragging the horse down the road. The sound of horse on gravel can be heard. Mort draws again on his pipe.
She drags the horse a couples yards away from the property.

                        MORT
 I can give you and yer beast a ride into town,
              if you need.

CUT TO:

EXT. DRIVING

The Gunslinger and Mort drive down the road in a pick-up. REVEAL that the horse is loosely tied to the roof of the truck.

CUT TO:

EXT. GENERAL STORE

The truck sits keenly outside the entrance to the store. The gunslinger climbs out of the car and begins to untie the horse.

                   GUNSLINGER
     Ah appreciate the ride, sir.

                    MORT
        Couldn't well let yuh drag a horse that far.
        Yew'd track blood 'urywhere and 'ttract bears.
           This time o' year lots o' bears 'round.

The gunslinger drags the horse off the truck
roof and between them with a thump.

                    MORT
              Well, ah'll be off.

Mort EXITS in a plume of exhaust.

The Gunslinger drags the horse toward the store
entrance.

CUT TO:

INT. GENERAL STORE

There's a counter, with a handmade sign that
says "HORSE REPAIR HERE".

The Gunslinger SLAMS the horse on the counter.
The clerk looks him over.

                    CLERK
        This may not be a pretty repair. (a beat)
            There's no shame in letting it go.

                    GUNSLINGER
        I'm naht givin' up. We're partners. Please
                repair as best ye can.

                    CLERK
        Very well. We'll have your horse in...some
        condition by the morning. You're welcome to
            rest at the nearest Inn till then.

                    GUNSLINGER
                Where'sat?

> CLERK
> (exhales, checks watch) It's about 30 miles up the road.

CUT TO:

EXT. PLAINS HOUSE-NIGHT
Wide shot. Mort is rocking in his chair. There's a sign that reads "INN".

Gunslinger enters the frame, ambling and in clear pain from the walk. She goes up to the porch.

> GUNSLINGER
> Kin ah get a room please?

CUT TO:

INT. PLAINS HOUSE-NIGHT

The Gunslinger is going to bed. She takes off her boot, and empties it, dumping out a LOT of blood. The shot of her pouring it goes on for a bit. We see the blood beginning to pool on the floor. She splish-splashes in it for a second.

Her boots thoroughly wrung out, the Gunslinger climbs into bed. The light is still on. She shoots it out, then blows out the smoking barrel.
CUT TO:

EXT. PLAINS HOUSE-MORNING

The Gunslinger stands outside, Mort rocks on the porch.

> GUNSLINGER
> OK, I'm off into town.

Mort nods.

Gunslinger starts to walk a few steps down the road and out of frame.

CUT TO:

EXT. GENERAL STORE

The gunslinger arrives, lightly limping, and heads to the front of the store.

The gunslinger catches her breath, and empties her boots. A TORRENT of blood, iron nails, tumbleweeds, etc rushes forth, soaking the entire storefront.

She knocks on the door.

>   CLERK(O.S.)
>   Meet me around back!

CUT TO:

EXT. GENERAL STORE BACK-MOMENTS LATER

The clerk walks the gunslinger to the stable on the side of the store.

>   CLERK (O.S.)
> Honestly, I'm surprised with how good he looks.
>   Surprised he made it, too.

REVEAL the horse, now an ABSOLUTE MESS of stitches, wooden limbs, and steampunk patchwork. It's eyes are sewn open in agony.

The Gunslinger is speechless.

                    CLERK
        Well, this'll be your total.
        The clerk hands her a receipt.

                    GUNSLINGER
              Thank...ye.

The gunslinger walks the horse away. It's gait is extremely uneven and labored- like walking on stilts, if one leg was 2 feet higher than the other.

                    GUNSLINGER
            C'mon. Giddy up a little!

Mechanical noises. An auto-tuned whinny. Then, a large BLAST OF STEAM.

                    GUNSLINGER
(avoiding being burnt) Ah, you mother fucker!

CUT TO:

EXT. THE ROAD-LATER

The gunslinger rides the horse, bouncing all over the place.
After a bit of riding, we see she is leaving a small but noticeable path of blood, dripping from her boots.

The gunslinger and the horse pass the plains house.

The gunslinger and the horse pass a sign that reads "BEAR COUNTRY."

CUT TO:

EXT. THE ROAD-DUSK

After a bit of riding, the gunslinger hears a

rustling in nearby bushes. Then a LOW GROWL. Alarmed, she jumps off of the horse, produces a gun and puts the handle in the horse's mouth.

                    GUNSLINGER
          Cover me. Fire if ah look like I'm in danger.

The gunslinger draws her gun.

She gingerly steps towards the bush, and trips. She loses the gun, and falls down the hill.

Her fall lands her directly in front of a BEAR.

She freezes. The bear notices her, and moves toward her.

The gunslinger draws her gun. The bear is about 20 feet away.

The bear draws a gun. They stare each other down.

The gunslinger FIRES, hitting the bear's hand, and destroying it.

The bear's pistol flies away.

The bear RUSHES FORWARD and swipes at the gunslinger- her pistol goes flying.

The gunslinger draws another gun, and the bear knocks it out of her hands. She draws another gun, and she's quickly disarmed. She draws a GRENADE, the bear knocks it away and there's a quick BURST OF LIGHT and EXPLOSION SFX.

The bear advances, and the gunslinger backs up.

GUNSHOT.

The bear stops it's advance, a smoking hole near its feet. The horse is holding the pistol in its mouth. The gunslinger and the horse make eye contact.

                    GUNSLINGER
                      Shoot it!

The bear grabs one of the gunslinger's discarded guns and points it at the horse.

                    GUNSLINGER
                    Don't you dare!

The bear and the horse hold their gaze. The horse glances at the gunslinger. It lets out a mechanical whinny.

The horse drops the gun, sending it tumbling towards the gunfighter.

GUNSHOT.

Horse scream. The horse falls, hit by the bear.

GUNSHOT.

The bear is hit.

GUNSHOT.

The gunslinger is hit. She drops her gun.

Shaking off the shot, the bear advances on her. She closes her eyes.

SCREEN GOES BLACK.

GUNSHOT.

A beat.

GUNSHOT. GUNSHOT. GUNSHOT.

The gunslinger opens her eyes. The bear trembles, then falls. Behind the bear, Mort holds his rifle.

                    MORT
    Told ye 'bout the Bears.

The gunslinger's vision goes hazy, and everything goes black again.

CUT TO:

INT. PLAINS HOUSE-MORNING

The gunslinger sits in the Inn bed, bandaged. Mort drops off a bowl of soup.

                    MORT
    Glad ye made it. Check out is 2PM.

Exit Mort.

Enter Clerk, covered in motor oil and horse bits.

                    CLERK
    Well, I managed to fix your horse again!

Clerk hands the gunslinger a bloody receipt.

                GUNSLINGER
    Ye think it'd be ok...if I saw 'im?

                  CLERK
    Oh yeah, sure.

Clerk produces a STEAMPUNK HORSE HEAD. It whirrs and makes horrible sci-fi noises, but the horse is alive, it's eyes sewn open.

                GUNSLINGER
                    Hm.

FADE TO:

EXT. PLAINS HOUSE-SUNSET
Mort and Clerk see off the gunslinger, who clutches the horse head under her arm.

                GUNSLINGER
   Well, ah'll be off. I reckon California s'about
      a 11 day walk from here. Thank ye for your
                 help everyone!

Mort takes a long draw from his pipe.

                   MORT
                  G'luck.

The gunslinger exits, into the sunset, doing a kind of weird horse-girl gallop skip. Music swells until-

                   CLERK
              Hey, wait a minute!

The clerk jogs toward her.

                   CLERK
            Take these, for your feet.

The clerk gives her FRESH SOCKS.

                   CLERK
            And for you, my friend.

The clerk stuffs a bunch of pain pills in the horses' mouth.

                   CLERK
                For the road.

                    GUNSLINGER
                 Much ablidged.

The clerk goes in to kiss the gunslinger.

                    GUNSLINGER
                 Ew! Jesus Christ!

She hits him in the nose with a pistol. He
yelps with pain.

The gunslinger skip/jumps into the sunset.

                      CLERK
            Can I at least know your name?

                    GUNSLINGER
                 (echoing) Fuck yoooou!

FADE TO BLACK

Twitter and Instagram: BensBryant
Youtube: YouTube.com/benbryant

Chapter 38

Love in the Time of Covid

By Andie Main

[MESSAGES ON A DATING APP]

DAVE: Oh hey, that's a cool shirt. I love Rites of Spring

CASEY: Oh thanks! Yeah they rule. What are you up to tonight?

DAVE: I mean what is there to do? Should i tell you i'm learning carpentry or be honest and tell you I'm watching Golden Girls.

CASEY: Haha yeah i mean same. I've been planning on writing the great american novel but I'm watching The Office. Again.

DAVE: So you're a comic huh? I've always wanted to try comedy

CASEY: Well I used to be a comic. Now I just tell jokes on my balcony into the void

DAVE: Who are you favs? I like Mitch Hedberg

CASEY: He's the number one comic people on this app tell me they like in order to impress me! lol *embarrassed emoji*

CASEY: I'm just teasing. He's cool. I like the alt stuff; Kyle Kinane, Rory Scovel, Maria Bamford- have you heard of any of them?

DAVE: Well no but I'll check em out for sure. I'm checking you out on YouTube right now though. You're great!

CASEY: Aw shucks thanks! Now I'm blushing a lil. If we weren't quarantined what would you be doing?

DAVE: Well I was/am a bartender so probably working. I work at Harvey's have you heard of it?

CASEY: No, but I spend all my time doing comedy so if there's not a show there I wouldn't have. I just moved here so...

DAVE: Lol yeah it's doesn't seem like your scene. I have to serve rich people and tell all the Karen's they've drank too much and they do not appreciate it!

CASEY: Haha oh damn. Karen is so entitled! Well I still have a job, so i gotta crash. It's been nice chatting with ya! G'night

DAVE: Night, pretty lady

CASEY: Haha shut up *blush*

Casey had been dating for almost a year after the big break up that led to her leaving her hometown and blowing up her whole prior life. It was a good move. She had been in her prior relationship for 15 years and that term about familiarity breeding contempt is very very real, so she was pretty sure that there was no such thing as love and we're all just doomed to repeat old patterns and the only thing she should focus on was telling jokes and maybe something cool could happen with her career that would make up for the fact that at this point she felt totally undateable after enduring so many trashy one night stands and flakes and people who just did not spark joy. She was realizing that going on a date is easy, but going on a third date is basically impossible.

It didn't help that she lived in Denver and everyone on the dating apps liked hiking. Casey did not give a fuck about hiking.

Dave looked promising. He had a scruffy punk look and maybe he's in a band? But what was the point of even messaging or swiping on someone in quarantine. It's just another thing to get excited about and ultimately disappointed by. Fuck he's super hot though. Casey couldn't help that she always went for dudes in bands. Maybe she wanted a guy to write a song about her? She wished she didn't keep meeting guys who were just fodder for her jokes.

It was like day 30 of lockdown? Who knows. The last shows before quarantine had a guilty vibe. She knew they all shouldn't be there, the audiences knew, so did the bartenders, but she knew she had to tell jokes while she could. Yeah, it's insane that she would risk her life for jokes but at that time Corona was known as Boomer Remover and only old assholes got it. And telling jokes was all she had. Her days were just working a shitty customer service job, but now that she didn't have that creative outlet her nights were spiraling into all of her depression's worst instincts. Who knew that canceling your plans, binging Netflix and ordering take out Chinese food was patriotic?

It was a victory when she managed to do some yoga and make a healthy meal before drinking it all away and numbly watching tv and obsessively checking her phone to see if anyone missed her or cared about her content. Her days were spent getting yelled at by customers and her nights were trying to erase it.

Casey started getting into the seediest part of Tinder; what she called Blackout Tinder. Enough booze and a few bowls into the night made her so agreeable. Buttstuff? Yeah why not. Water play? Uh maybe? She'd wake up to an inbox of bad jokes, dubious pick up lines and occasionally rapey shit. Drinking all night and feeling gross about an inbox was actually a pretty good substitute for waking up next to one of these potential dates, so maybe isolation wasn't that bad. It was a lot more efficient to wake up to 2 or 3 virtual encounters you're grossed out by than one person a night every week. It was just so weird how much everyone still wanted to connect with each other although it was also potentially fatal. How dystopian.

Was this true before Covid? Is it too heavy handed for the narrator, drunk on vodka and her own hubris to dwell on? Naw. Shit's all fucked. Let's be self indulgent. The author, who let's not doubt is definitely not just writing this story as a thinly veiled projection of her own life onto a character who is not at all dissimilar, predicts that post-corona, in three years, once we're settled back into whatever routine is going to be the new normal? When humans aren't hoarding toilet paper and everyone has gotten used to mass graves and you can go back to a bar, it's gonna be one or two weeks of empathy, and then we'll be back to our same bullshit.

DAVE: Hey girl, how was your day?

CASEY Oh hi Dave! Just another forgettable night staring at the void, how about you?

DAVE: Same. Just got done mixing some tracks from my band, which is the most productive thing I've done all day. Otherwise i watched Planet Earth and cried about baby penguins getting eaten by seals. Am I not supposed to admit that?

CASEY: Hahahaa OMG I have spent many a night drinking wine and crying over how i love penguins and orcas and why can't they get along?? Wanna text? I hate how limited this app is

DAVE: Sure xxx-xxx-xxxx

DAVE: So why are you single?

CASEY: Just broke off a long term relationship. It was a positive midlife crisis. Blew everything up and I moved out here. It was the best change I could have made. You?

DAVE: I dunno. I hate small talk so i thought i'd get into it.

CASEY: Yeah me too. Especially right now. What are we doing talking? Like what's the point of getting to know someone?

DAVE: Oh I dunno i like being teased

CASEY: Yeah?

DAVE: I wanna see more of you

CASEY: Mmmmm ok like what

DAVE: You know

CASEY: Oh do i? How do i know you won't spread my photos around when i get famous

DAVE: Are you gonna get famous?

CASEY: Oh i dunno is your band?

DAVE: Nope.

CASEY: Same.

DAVE: *sends a photo*
You like?

CASEY: Mmmm oh fuck, yeah what's not to like

DAVE: I wanna see you

CASEY: See me do what

DAVE: Anything without your shirt on

CASEY: Like doing laundry, or picking my nose haha

DAVE: Are you telling jokes right now while I'm so hard?

CASEY: *sends photo*

DAVE: Oh you are a dirty little girl aren't you

CASEY: Sir, I will have you know I'm a nasty woman and i get shit done #feminism

DAVE: I wanna put my huge throbbing dick in between those feminist tittes

Casey pulled back for a moment, this wasn't her style, but she kept playing along since she was wasted and had nothing else for entertainment...

CASEY: Haha well hopefully we can some day but

DAVE: But what?

CASEY: But what about Quarantine? Also, you know, chemistry or whatever

DAVE: I'm not trying to pressure you into anything, but also i want to know you. We have a good match right now cuz i've looked up your whole deal. I heard your album, your podcast.

I'm in. Let's see if you are too

CASEY: WELL FUCK

DAVE: I know right?

CASEY:Gimme some time, idk

DAVE: What?

CASEY: OK if you kill me my friends are gonna be furious. Gotta crash, working tomorrow.

DAVE: Ok pretty lady. I look forward to hearing from you. I loved your Werner Herzog bit

CASEY: OHH GOD haha SHUT UP

Casey woke up and read those messages again and again. How was her boob pic? Decent? Did she still have nice boobs at 39? What's up with that dick pic. Haha it was awesome. And he likes her comedy? wow wow woooow. But why is he into her for real? Casey had a natural distrust of anyone who actually showed interest since like, if she was flawed, and they were into her, they were flawed too.

She texted with her best friend and of course she said "DUDE YOU ARE LOVABLE NOW GO GET SOME LOVE IN THE TIME OF CORONA! If you're not hanging in large groups it's FIIIIIINE. Baskin Robbins is open right now. YOUR ORGASM IS MORE ESSENTIAL OK"

Casey couldn't argue that logic.

She texted Dave that night just a simple

CASEY: Hey

DAVE: Hey girl what's up?

CASEY: Just lonely and kind drunk, like always, you?

DAVE: Haha i've had a few beers but i'm chillin. You want some company?

CASEY: Yeah, i kinda do. But is this ok? Like, i'm not even worried about meeting a virtual stranger at my house but i don't think tinder hookups are "essential" rn.

DAVE: Are you sure that I'm not an essential worker?

CASEY: Well you were a bartender soooo

DAVE: Ouch

CASEY: Haha. Are you coming over?

DAVE: Oh yeah

CASEY: K cool here's my address

DAVE: What if we just fuckin went for it as soon as i walked inside

CASEY: Omg mmmm maybe?

DAVE: I've never done that before, have you? I think it'd be so hot

CASEY: I mean, if i told i had, would you hold it against me?

DAVE: First of all, great band, secondly YES

CASEY: OK well shut up and get over here

Dave was a little beyond 3 beers but he didn't really give a fuck. He hadn't left his house for days and hadn't gotten laid for weeks. He could see that Casey was sexy, but not like sexy enough for him to have to work very hard to get her. She was sexy in that way where they both knew that she would put up with his bullshit. Oh yes, it turns out that Dave is the villain in this story.

As he got out of the Lyft he texted "i'm five min away" just so he could have another edge on her. Casey texted back "K!" right as he knocked on her door

Casey was taken off guard and slightly annoyed, and opened the door with her brows furrowed.

"Dave?"

"Hi baby"

Dave leaned in for a wet sloppy whiskey infused kiss, and Casey went for it, even though it wasn't what she actually wanted. If she was gonna be honest? Maybe she did want to settle down and create a life with another person again. Maybe she did want someone t text her first, maybe they knew her favorite bands and they had inside jokes… but this was going to be just another hook up. She could tell by the way he just grabbed her ass right then.

They grinded against each other and grabbed each other and even though, on paper, this could've been so hot, Casey just could not find a point of passion to keep escalating. This was stupid. It was dangerous. And he wasn't a great kisser. It felt like her mouth was being fucked with a limp dick. Who taught this dude how to kiss?

Casey hadn't had good sex in maybe ever? She was used to going through the motions. Her early years on stage bombing as a new comic also made her a good liar, pretending everything was going well when it so clearly wasn't.. So when he guided her hand to his dick she acquiesced, and gave it a few tugs under his pants. BTW, this was all within 2 minutes of opening the door. They were still standing, his tongue was still throatfucking her, and now she had a limp dick of undetermined size in her hand, and she was just completely not turned on.

"Ok hey hey hold on"

She pushed him away and saw a pure expression on his face of clear annoyance, not concern. How could he be annoyed? She was gonna be the one who has to deal with this douchebaggery.

He was the one in her house. FUCK. Also, doing the mental trigonometry of how lousy this dude smelled, like Jack Daniels, combined with his assumption that she wanted it, no matter what it was, and OH GOD CASEY- you never even checked out his band! It could be fuckin pop-punk! HE COULD PLAY TRUMPET IN A SKA BAND FOR ALL YOU KNOW.

Also, by the way, remember how you went through a traumatic procedure to get an IUD, so that your pussy could be ready for men, and how all this man did to get ready for you is to just exist? Like, if he knew he wasnt gonna be able to get hard, he coulda taken a pill. All Casey had to do was put wires in her guts and feel a pain that was comparable to child birth.

Casey took his hand off of him. He put it back on. She felt what could best be described as a dick which dreamed, some day, to achieve a boner, but it wasn't gonna be with her tonight. Good luck to you, hot guy with a great head of hair and no clue.

Still standing before her door, limpish cock still in her hand, her door knob in the other, Casey opened it, and pushed Dave, gently, outside. The last time she ever saw his sharp cheekbones and ruffled bad boy ironic mullet was as she closed and locked the door. She heard him yell "YOU FAT BITCH" as she blocked him on tinder and her phone.

Two weeks later, she got a dry cough, a sore throat, and couldn't taste her food. It was still better than sucking off another fuck boy.

Twitter and Instagram: AndieMain
Podcast: PETA - People Enjoying Terrible Accidents
(vegetarians making fun of people who have been murdered by animals)

Teeny Tiny Chapter 39

Hi again, Reader!

Remember me? It's old Sarah Benson from the beginning of the book (and that one part!) all those chapters ago. Although it feels far away, it's only separated from this sentence by mere inches of paper! And yet somehow it seems like we've been on a whole *journey* together.

I just wanted to say a quick little goodbye and congratulations! You finished a whole book. Go treat yourself, Reader, you deserve it! (Have some cake! Shake a snow-globe! Tie your shoes with a slightly different knot! Really *celebrate*.)

Thank you for being a part of a project that made all of us feel a little closer during a lonely time. If you do ever feel lonely again, pick up this book and give it a hug. Or read it. Or call your friends and/or family and tell them you love them. (Probably do that first.)

I guess I better mosey on out of here pretty soon. You know, for the sake of "economy of words" and whatnot.

Sending some love and gratitude from a different place and time!

Your ~~friend~~ ~~buddy~~ ~~pal~~ friend,

[imagine a beautiful, soulful signature here]

Sarah

For updates on live comedy around Colorado (especially once the pandemic ends!) check out 5280comedy.com.

Made in the USA
Monee, IL
22 July 2020